AR Quiz # 115073
BL: 5.4
AR Pts: 8.0

W9-BBF-954

HAYNER PUBLIC LIBRARY DISTRICT
ALTON, ILLINOIS

OVERDUES .10 PER DAY MAXIMUM FINE
COST OF BOOKS. LOST OR DAMAGED
BOOKS ADDITIONAL $5.00 SERVICE CHARGE.

The Middle of

SOMEWHERE

J. B. CHEANEY

Alfred A. Knopf
NEW YORK

HAYNER PUBLIC LIBRARY DISTRICT
ALTON, ILLINOIS

NEBRASKA

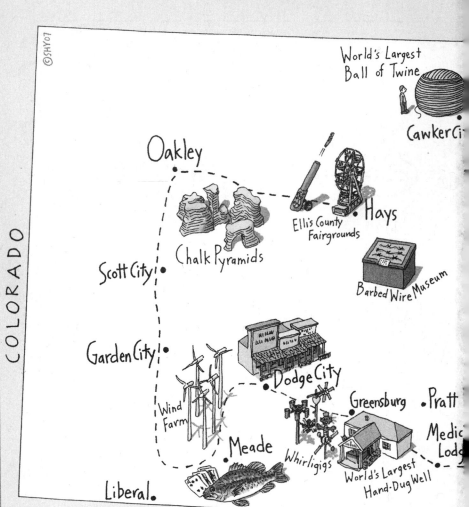

©SHY07

COLORADO

World's Largest
Ball of Twine

Cawker Ci

Oakley

Ellis County
Fairgrounds

Hays

Chalk Pyramids

Scott City

Barbed Wire Museum

Garden City

Dodge City

Greensburg

Pratt

Medic
Lodg

Wind
Farm

Meade

Whirligigs

World's Largest
Hand-Dug Well

Liberal

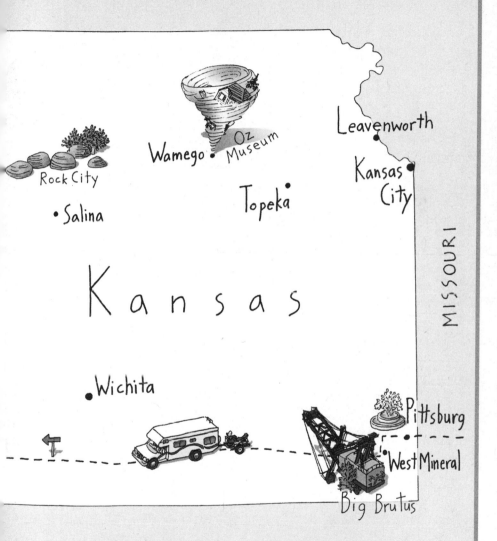

Rock City

Salina

Wamego
Oz Museum

Topeka

Leavenworth

Kansas City

MISSOURI

K a n s a s

Wichita

Pittsburg

West Mineral

Big Brutus

OKLAHOMA

THIS IS A BORZOI BOOK PUBLISHED BY ALFRED A. KNOPF

This is a work of fiction. Names, characters, places, and incidents either are the product of the author's imagination or are used fictitiously. Any resemblance to actual persons, living or dead, events, or locales is entirely coincidental.

Text copyright © 2007 by J. B. Cheaney
Map copyright © 2007 by Susan Hunt Yule
Photo p. 84 copyright © Dave Nance
Photo p. 132 copyright © Keith Stokes

All rights reserved.

Published in the United States by Alfred A. Knopf, an imprint of Random House Children's Books, a division of Random House, Inc., New York.

KNOPF, BORZOI BOOKS, and the colophon are registered trademarks of Random House, Inc.

www.randomhouse.com/kids

Educators and librarians, for a variety of teaching tools, visit us at www.randomhouse.com/teachers

Library of Congress Cataloging-in-Publication Data
Cheaney, J. B.
The middle of somewhere / J. B. Cheaney. — 1st ed.
p. cm.
SUMMARY: Twelve-year-old Ronnie loves organization, especially because her brother has attention-deficit hyperactivity disorder, but traveling with their grandfather who is investigating wind power in Kansas brings some pleasant, if chaotic, surprises.
ISBN 978-0-375-83790-6 (trade) — ISBN 978-0-375-93790-3 (lib. bdg.)
[1. Automobile travel—Fiction. 2. Brothers and sisters—Fiction.
3. Grandfathers—Fiction. 4. Attention-deficit hyperactivity disorder—Fiction.
5. Kansas—Fiction.] I. Title.
PZ7.C3985Mid 2007
[Fic]—dc22
2006029202

Printed in the United States of America

May 2007

10 9 8 7 6 5 4 3 2 1

First Edition

JF
CHE

617709 313

To Doug:
who hates sudden moves,
loud noises,
and surprises.
Surprise!

Don't let life's little surprises get you down.
Expect the unexpected! Remember, there's always
a Plan B.

—Kent Clark,
Seize the Way:
Ten Weeks to SuperSize Your Life!

None of this that I'm about to tell you would have happened if my mother hadn't found that squirrel in the toilet.

Kent Clark says that life is full of surprises. This particular surprise started with my brother leaving the front door open again, which he's not supposed to do because there's a big tear in the storm-door screen that my mother never got around to having fixed.

When the squirrel got in, my brother was the first to go nuts. My mother went nuts right after, because when she's having one of her Bad Days it doesn't take much. Then the squirrel went nuts because—but let me back up.

It was the first Saturday morning in June. My brother—whose name is Gerald but we've always called him "Gee"—was sprawled on the floor in the living room watching cartoons. All of a sudden, a fuzzy tail flickered across the screen. Next minute, the furry little animal attached to the tail had whipped around on top of the TV and was staring my brother right in the face. Both were equally shocked, I'm sure, but Gee was the one who screamed. Then he threw what was closest to hand, which happened to be a bowl of Cheerios, and we were off to the races.

With Gee leaping and lunging after him, the squirrel zoomed all the way around the living room twice before discovering the kitchen door. His squirrelly brain probably leapt with joy—*Ah, escape hatch!*—as he shot through the opening.

Only to be confronted with another screaming person: my mother. She hadn't been much alarmed when Gee let loose, because Gee screaming is no big deal. But a small, four-legged mammal on the counter, knocking spoons to the floor and making tracks right through the pancakes on the griddle—that's a big deal. "Ronniiie!" she yelled.

Ronnie is me, Veronica Sparks. At that exact moment, I was on the bed in my room reading a copy of *Architectural Digest* from the library. Or maybe "reading" isn't the best word for poring over diagrams of how to organize a closet, which was my current project. That jangly tone in my mother's "Ronniiie!" made the magazine jump out of my hands and dive to the floor. Something big was going down.

And when I reached the kitchen door, it hurled itself at me: a reddish-gray ball of fur with a twirly tail and beady eyes and toothy mouth stretched wide like a little bear trap, landing right on my chest!

Then *I* screamed, which those who know me will agree is a *very* rare occurrence.

The squirrel leapt off my chest as quick as he'd leapt on. Next, a wild chase with dialogue to match.

ME: Open the back door and shoo him out!

MAMA: I tried that, but whenever I make a move he goes berserk!

ME: So?! He's not going any berserker! I'll chase him your way!

GEE: Aiieee!

MAMA: Don't let him get near the fan!

ME: I'll head him off!

GEE: Ow! Ow! Ow! (Which he yells sometimes, not because he's hurt but because it's an easy yell to do over and over.)

MAMA: Okay, now—oh *no!*

The "oh *no*" was because even though our peppy little visitor got safely through the door, it was the wrong door—back into the living room, with a little squad of Sparkses (that's us) in hot pursuit.

If I'd thought, while still on my bed looking over *Architectural Digest, Hmmm, that particular tone in my mother's voice probably means that some wild animal is loose in the house. Therefore, on my way to the kitchen I'll open the storm door in the living room, just in case the critter heads that way*—if such thoughts had run through my head at that point, tragedy could have been avoided. But I'm not so good at handling life's little surprises yet.

The squirrel saw daylight through the storm door and slammed his panicky body against it, but he missed the hole in the screen that got him into this mess in the first place. Bouncing off the screen, he spun around, getting even more confused, then headed for the hallway.

The straightest route from the hall led into my room, which at the moment was nothing but walls and corners. I was reorganizing, so all my stuff was piled in the middle of the floor: no posters, shelves, or anything to break up the monotony. That squirrel got up such a speed he was running sideways on the wall, like some hotshot skateboarder. But after twice around, he careened back into the hall and headed for my mother's bedroom.

Mama never reorganizes. And she never throws anything away. Her room always looked like an explosion in Granny's Drawers Antique Mall (where some of the stuff came from): two dressers, two sewing machines, stacks of plastic storage boxes, a wardrobe with its door hanging open, an empty birdcage, and (somewhere) a bed. And that's only the big stuff. To a squirrel, it must have looked like hideaway heaven, after bare-wall hell. He dived in and disappeared.

We heard some crackles and rustles, but soon not even that. In the sudden quiet, the three of us stared at each other. "All right," Mama said grimly. "He's in here *somewhere*. Gee, don't move. Ronnie and I'll flush him out."

So the two of us went on patrol while Gee stayed by the door. He couldn't just *stay*, though—he kept squatting down to peer under furniture, chanting, "Squirrel-ly. Squirr-rel-ly." We had to keep telling him to quit so we could listen for movement. For five minutes at least, we crept around like jungle commandos searching for the enemy spy—tiptoe to the hat rack; stop and listen. Peek under the bed; stop and listen. And try not to think of a screaming kamikaze rodent leaping from behind the rolls of gift wrap to latch on to your nose.

Finally, Mom straightened up and wiped the sweat off

her forehead with a mighty sigh. "This is the last thing I need today. Rent's due, A/C's broken, and I've *got* to clean up this room. But if I don't get to the bathroom right now, I'm gonna pop." She eased around the sewing-machine table. "Keep a watch, Ronnie. If that nasty rodent makes a move, chase him *out*."

Gee leapt at her, knocking over a pile of plastic storage bins. "Don't go, Mama!"

She got ahold of her temper and held him off. "It's just to the bathroom, sugar. Help your sister, okay?" As her steps creaked into the hall, my brother slipped over and grabbed my hand. We tiptoed toward the closet.

Then from the bathroom came a hair-raising screech, followed by a squeak, and finally a WHAM!

When we got to the bathroom door, still holding hands, the sight struck us both at the same time: Mama flat on the floor with one leg twisted to the side. Hanging over the edge of the toilet seat was something that looked exactly like a squirrel tail.

Of course Gee started screaming again. Meanwhile, my mother was moaning in pain, so it took a while to sort out what happened.

There's a hole in the wall between my mother's room and the bathroom. How it got there is anybody's guess, but my guess is that somebody who used to live here had a temper and wore steel-toed boots. The hole made a crooked tepee shape in the bedroom wall and a little boot-toe shape in the bathroom, which you wouldn't think a grown-up squirrel could get through. But as I learned that day, there's not much to them but fur.

Our squirrel must've thought his luck had changed when he found an escape hatch. And while he sat on the tile floor catching his breath, his little heart pattering like a snare drum, he must have picked up the scent of water. A life-or-death chase over hill and dale and hot skillet can make a critter thirsty.

So he nosed down into the toilet—which was easy, since Gee left the seat up again—only to find that there was no nosing out. The harder he scurried, the farther he sank, until his little head was wedged into the inlet hole and he was all the way drowned. My mother came in right after.

The screech we heard was her shock at Rocky the Flying Squirrel's tragic end. The squeak was her slipping on the wet tile floor, and the thump was her fall. It was a loud thump, because my mother—though cute as a bug with her curly dark hair and bright blue eyes—is a bit on the heavy side.

So our squirrel problem was solved, but now we had a Mama problem. Which turned out to be a whole lot worse. I didn't know how much worse until I tried to help her up and she screamed in pain: "Call 911!" Gee yelled the same, as though I hadn't heard it the first time. (A lot of yelling goes on in our house.)

The operator dispatched an ambulance and transferred me to the hospital, where the nurse on duty told me to put a pillow under Mama's head but not to move her or apply any pressure to the leg or knee. "What's that noise in the background?" she asked.

"That's my brother. He's ADHD. Once he gets wound up he's hard to unwind."

"Well, see what you can do," she said. "That can't be helpful."

No kidding, thought I as I thanked her and hung up.

Our little town is fifteen miles from the nearest hospital—which never seemed very far before, but try waiting for the ambulance to arrive while keeping your injured mother comfortable and your hyper little brother quiet. Mama got herself under control, but she couldn't help crying because her leg hurt so bad. I couldn't help crying a little, too, and since I hardly ever cry, that got Gee going again. The only thing that cheered him up, finally, was getting an ambulance ride to the hospital. And even then, he kept popping up to rattle equipment and ask ADHD questions—the kind that never wait for answers—until the medic suggested, "Kid, do you want a shot of what we gave your mom?"

After that, our day got long and boring. I won't go into all the details, except that Mama had to have emergency knee surgery and somebody had to figure out who would pay for it and who would take care of us while she was recuperating. That meant a long meeting with a lady with a stack of file folders who met us in one of those tiny offices that hospital architects seem to stick anywhere there's extra space. After some opening chitchat, she asked, "Okay, Ronnie, where's your dad?"

"In heaven," I said.

The lady put down her pen, heaved a big sigh, and gave

me a sympathetic look, along with a moment of silence. "I'm sorry to hear that."

"Sorry he's in heaven?"

"No, I mean—" She raised her voice to carry outside to the lobby, where Gee was amusing himself. "Gerald, honey, please stop playing with the automatic doors." Back to me: "How long ago was your father—I mean, did he—?"

"Five years. I was seven. I'm twelve now." That was more about me than him, but I don't like to talk about him much. He was a long-haul truck driver, big and strong and funny. Hugging him was like throwing your arms round a stout oak tree. One icy night in January he stopped on the highway near Chicago to help a lady change a flat tire. While he was wrenching lug nuts off the tire, he got hit by a chicken truck. That may sound funny, getting hit by a chicken truck. Most people think that anything with chickens in it has to be funny. But I don't.

The lady, whose name tag read L. DANIELS, picked up her pen. "So who's the next of kin that lives closest to you?"

"My grandfather, probably. My mother's dad. John Q. Hazeltine."

"Gerald—don't even *think* about climbing those drapes. And where does he live?"

"On the road." She looked at me. "No, really, he doesn't settle anyplace. He's got this old camper and lots of business on the road. He stops by every now and then to see us."

"But isn't there some way you can reach him in emergencies?"

"Emergencies, no. But we send Christmas cards and

changes of address to the Happy Trails Travel Court in Muleshoe, Texas. That's his winter headquarters."

"But summer just started, so he won't be there?"

"No, ma'am."

"What about your other grandparents? Gerald! Stop that!"

I gave her the whole family history: how my dad's father had passed away and his mother was a missionary in Warsaw, Poland, and how my grandmother on Mama's side, the one who was no longer married to John Q. Hazeltine, lived in a gated retirement community in Florida that she only left to go on cruises with her second husband. L. Daniels wrote in the folder for a long time, probably about what a hopeless family we were. She froze up when Gee bounced into the office, but all he did was flop down in the chair next to mine, keel over with his head in my lap, and fall asleep. I mean, *fall* asleep, like from the top of a cliff or something.

"He sleeps hard," I said.

Gee was still zonked out an hour later when the surgeon stopped by to tell me the operation was successful but Mama would have to stay off her feet for at least a month. "You look like you'd be a big help around the house, right?" I just nodded—that's the story of my life so far, though I'm working on Plan B.

"We'll release her tomorrow if there's a responsible adult at home to help you."

I nodded again, mentally flipping through my short list of responsible adults. We've only lived in Partly, Missouri—seriously, that's the name of the town—since

February and don't have that many friends yet. Lyddie McIntyre was probably the best option. She's an old buddy of Mama's who convinced her to move to Partly because it was cheaper than living in the Kansas City area and the school here needed another cafeteria worker.

When Mama got out of surgery and felt clearheaded enough to make the call, Lyddie agreed to be our responsible adult.

That's how my summer vacation started. If it hadn't been for Kent Clark, I would have been really bummed about it.

He's the author of this paperback book I picked up in the dentist's office last fall: *Seize the Way: Ten Weeks to SuperSize Your Life!* The chapters had titles like "Finding the Silver Lining" and "Row the Flow." The pages were full of bullet points and checklists and short- and long-term goals. A little voice inside my head whispered, *Seize the book!* Since it didn't seem to belong to anybody, I slipped it in my jacket pocket and read almost all of it that night while the numbness was wearing off my back molars. By bedtime, I'd made my very first list of long-term goals:

1. Buy a car.
2. Start a business in high school (or sooner), save money.
3. After graduation, travel for one year.
4. College? (Decide in high school.)
5. Start using my full name.

I like "Veronica" but never liked "Ronnie." However, as long as you're underage, who's going to call you with four syllables when they can do it with two?

Speaking of names, in the prologue of his book, Kent Clark makes a big deal of his real actual name being Kent Clark—which didn't seem worth making a big deal about until I remembered *Clark Kent*. Aha: SuperMan, SuperSize. Which is pretty lame, but it's a super book— I've learned not only how to Row the Flow, but also how to Game My Goals and Affirmatize My Attitude.

Still, anybody's attitude would take a hit if they had to leave their mother in the hospital and come home to a torn-up house with pancake-batter tracks in the kitchen and a drowned squirrel in the toilet.

Lyddie stuck around for a couple hours to help clean up and stop Gee from denting our car with a shovel while playing Knight's Tale. (This was after she stopped him from digging up Mama's petunia bed to make a grave for Rocky.) "Whew" was her comment after plopping him in front of the TV with a bowl of popcorn. "Is he always like this?" All our friends get around to that question sooner or later.

"In a little bit," she went on, "I have to run down to Springfield for my grandson's birthday party, but I'll check on you when I get back. And of course I'll be here tomorrow morning to take you to the hospital to get your mom. Will you guys be okay?"

"Sure," I said. Lyddie was playing responsible adult, but the real responsibility around here was mine.

Row the Flow: that is, find the direction your life is

going anyway and figure out how to make it suit your goals. But my life was flowing in a seriously weird direction. How'd I flow into this dinky little town with institutions called Partly School and Partly Baptist Church, etc.? Would that make me partly-Veronica for the rest of my life?

What would it take, I wondered while scrubbing the last of the pancake batter off the kitchen wall, to change direction altogether? That's one reason my first long-term goal was buying a car: to whoosh me somewhere else if I didn't like where I was. But "long-term" meant at least three years in the future. For now I was stuck in the family boat.

Figuring out how to row it was beyond me after an evening of cleanup that took twice as long with Gee "helping." When my head hit the pillow that night, I sank like a rock.

Unbeknownst to me, though, the poky current of my life was about to hit the rapids!

CHAPTER
2

Destiny is not something that happens to you—
it's something you make happen!

—Kent Clark,
Seize the Way

Kent Clark says that one way to hear destiny knocking is to notice when two unusual events happen *at the same time.* One unusual event, all by itself, can flare up and then just fade away. But when two of them happen together, they can stir up a crazy kind of energy that just keeps popping and fizzing. So the first unusual event of my summer destiny was Mama falling in the bathroom and busting up her knee. The second happened the very next morning.

I was in the middle of a dream where Gee and I were in the freshwater aquarium at Bass Pro Outdoor World. It was feeding time and the usual crowd had gathered to watch the catfish and largemouth bass dart for those lumps of processed food thrown out by the fish feeder. Gee was darting, too, because being with the fish inspired him to act "fishy." The feeder thought it was funny. He kept throwing nuggets my brother's way and Gee kept diving for them and I was afraid he'd drown. The crowd was laughing—like the kids at school, when Gee does something off the wall and they don't know how to react. "Stop it!" I yelled in my dream. "Don't encourage him!" At the shooting gallery near the aquarium, somebody kept scoring targets with a loud buzz that got on my nerves.

It was one of those dreams that make you wake up exhausted. Especially when you wake up to your little brother bouncing on your stomach, shouting, "Ronnie! There's somebody at the door!"

My alarm clock said seven—way too early to wake up on a Sunday morning. I threw off the covers, and Gee along with them, wrapped myself up in a bathrobe, and shuffled into the living room. Mama has told us over and over not to open the door to strangers, but my brain was still swimming with the fish. I turned the dead bolt and flung the door wide open as if to say, "Welcome! Come in and steal all I have and don't forget to take my little brother for ransom!"

The first thing that caught my squinchy eyes was not the man on the porch but the slick maroon-and-white RV in our driveway. Me and RVs go way back, and this one looked so new I could almost smell it from the porch. Then I noticed gold letters on the cab door:

JOHN Q. (JACK) HAZELTINE
WIND PROSPECTOR
"POWER FROM THE SKY"

"Ronnie!" exclaimed my grandfather. "Long time no see!"

I'd better explain about John Q. Hazeltine, better known as Jack.

He doesn't really look like a grandpa, and I get the idea he doesn't think of himself as one, either. Nobody calls him "Grandpa," that's for sure. I think he'd be okay with us

calling him "Jack," but Mama put her foot down on that.
She says anybody can be Jack, but we've only got one
grandfather. So we compromised on "Pop."

He's tallish and thinnish, with crinkly blue eyes like
Mama's and the leathery skin of somebody who's outside a
lot. He wears a broad-brimmed hat—suede in the winter
and straw in the summer—to keep the sun out of his eyes,
but also to cover his bald spot. At least, that's Mama's
opinion. And he rides a motorcycle, an old Yamaha; I could
see the little bike trailer attached to the RV.

What I told L. Daniels was true: he pretty much lived
on the road, but not as a drifter. He was a man with a plan.
Every time we saw or heard from him, he was working on
a new business, usually based on some awesome scientific
discovery that took a long time to explain. It was always
something "on the cutting edge," meaning you couldn't just
go down to Wal-Mart and buy it.

A couple of years ago, for instance, he was selling elec-
tromagnets to farmers, on the principle that reversing the
magnetic poles in the field would increase crop yields by
at least 50 percent. Before that, it was special drinking
glasses and coffee mugs that made the electrons in water
spin the opposite direction from what they usually spun.
Drinking opposite-spinning electrons was supposed to
cure cancer and clear up zits and fix everything in between.

Whatever he sold, he never stayed in the same place for
long. Mama explained it this way: "He's got an itchy right
foot. It's always feeling for the accelerator."

Before now, though, the accelerator was attached to a
dusty gray pickup with an old camper riding it like a wart

on a toe. Not the bright new RV that had his own name painted on the door. He saw my eyes lingering on its smooth lines and shiny body. "Like my new wheels? Wait'll you hear the story. Where's your mother?"

When I looked back from the vehicle to him, he'd kind of taken on a bright new gleam himself. "Well, that's a story, too. Come on in, Pop."

Every time he comes in (every time I remember, at least), two things happen—Gee leaps out screaming from behind a door or a piece of furniture and wraps himself around Pop's body. And the man jumps a foot and gives Gee a shake and says, "Don't you *ever* do that again!" Pop hates sudden moves and loud noises. Also surprises, although since this happens every time, it wasn't technically a surprise.

In the usual scenario, Mama comes bustling out of the kitchen with a big smile and a friendly put-down, like, "Look what the cat drug in!" Except that didn't happen this time, of course.

So when the dust settled after Gee's ambush, Pop asked again, "Where's your mother?" While I told him, Pop frowned. When I finished, he smiled. "How's that for timing? Just when you need me, I'm here. Ronnie, call that lady and tell her she won't have to take you to the hospital. When do we have to be there? Eleven? That gives us a few hours—let's put this house in order. Her bedroom's a wreck, right? Always is. We'll clear a path to the bed. Hey, Gee—buddy" (my brother was a little pouty after being yelled at) "gimme five."

Being head of the family for the last twelve hours had

taken its toll on me—there's supersize and then there's way outtasize. So when my next of kin sailed in and masterfully took control, I almost burst into tears.

But instead, I burst into activity.

In a couple hours, the kitchen and living room were neat as a pin, and Mama's bedroom, though still chaotic, was organized chaos. "Like the U.S. government," Pop said when I mentioned it.

We thought alike: when he said, "Let's move her sewing machine to the corner and stack all her storage bins here," it was exactly what I would have done. When a pile of hatboxes toppled over and hit him on the head, he found a better place to put them. He made the same kind of busywork jobs for Gee that I often did, just to keep him out of our way while we did the real thing.

I'd never known Pop that well before; he'd never stuck around long enough. But after a few hours, I was starting not just to know him, but also to look up to him.

"Now!" he said finally, shaking the dust mop out the back door. "It's time to bring your mother home from the hospital in style."

"In style" meant in a Coachman Freedom RV: Chevy chassis and motor, twenty-three and a half feet long, space to comfortably sleep four, with a thirty-two-gallon fresh-water tank and a six-gallon water heater, reclining cockpit seats, oak cabinets, six-speaker AM/FM and CD player, smoke and CO_2 detectors, microwave, three-burner range, shower—

"And a itty-bitty toilet!" Gee exclaimed, checking it out. "I have to go!"

Pop said no, so after a short trip to our own bathroom we were on the road, headed for the hospital—though I wished the trip could be a little longer, like coast to coast. Even a fifteen-mile ride in the reclining swivel seat made me feel like I was rolling along in a palace. "How'd you get it, Pop?" I asked once we'd turned onto the highway and reached cruising speed. "I mean . . ." None of his next-big-thing businesses had exactly paid off for him, but I didn't know how to tactfully suggest—

"Yeah!" Gee shouted from the dinette. "Your old camper was a piece of junk!"

So much for tact. He'd heard that from Mama—one of those statements kids aren't supposed to repeat. But Pop just chuckled. "That's a story for after we pick up your mother. Can't wait to see her face."

Mama's face, when she saw him, went still and gray as Mount Rushmore: no remarks about what the cat drug in. It must have been from shock, though, because by the time we pushed her out through the big glass doors in a borrowed wheelchair, she was starting to perk up. And when she caught sight of the Coachman, she gasped out loud. "Dad! Where did *that* come from?"

He promised again to tell us later. For the ride home, he converted the dinette seat to a bed and hauled out extra pillows to prop up Mama so she could watch the scenery. He even took the long way, giving Gee plenty of time to get a can of Coke out of the little fridge and carefully pour it into a plastic cup for Mama and wash it out in the sink when she was done. As a reward for all that work, he got to go in the itty-bitty toilet—"Just this once," Pop said.

For me, it was like a dream. Seriously. Every year at the state fair, I do my duty and take Gee through the livestock barns and petting zoo—but the high point for me, even better than the rides, is the RV lot. I go through every single one, even though Gee gets bored really quick and begs for another spin on the Scrambler. I pick up all the brochures and study the plans when I get home and imagine how cool it would be just to get in and go. And here I was, in an RV, just going.

Maybe in a year or two, I could talk Pop into taking me someplace. For now I kept pointing him down side roads, hoping he'd get lost and we could wander for a few hours. But his sense of direction is a lot better than mine, meaning we were home in forty minutes.

Mama was tired again, so she took a nap in her less-cluttered bedroom. During the afternoon, our neighbor Mrs. Tracy brought over a strawberry-rhubarb pie, and soon after Lyddie knocked on the door with a big pot of chili. Even Mr. Harper, principal of Partly School, came by with a coffee cake from the supermarket bakery. He was the only one to ask about the logo on the truck door: "'Power from the Sky'? What does that mean, Mr. Hazeltine?"

"Just call me Jack, Bob. That means electrical generation from natural, renewable atmospheric sources. In a word, wind power."

That was two words, but never mind—little did I know they meant a stiff breeze of destiny for me! Meanwhile, Mr. Harper asked, "But what does 'wind prospecting' involve?"

Bad move—Pop could easily go on for twice the amount of time needed to explain anything. After five minutes, you either got it or you didn't, but he'd keep going regardless. I caught the gist of it: Pop was riding the headwinds—literally—of the next stage in power generation. His work as a prospector was to scout likely places for setting up wind farms. It sounded like another weird science project at first, like crop magnets or reversed electrons—until Pop mentioned getting a grant from some university in Kansas. *Hmm,* thought I, *could he really be on to something this time?*

After all the company left, we rearranged the furniture in the living room to make a convalescent center. Once Mama was settled on the couch, with pillows to prop up all her sore parts, I spread a tablecloth on the floor and we gathered around for a picnic supper of chili and coffee cake. Gee ate them together.

Before sitting on the floor, Pop went out to the RV and brought back one of those plastic medicine organizers with compartments for every day of the week. "Wow, you take a lot of pills!" Gee exclaimed.

"Not pills," Pop corrected. "Supplements. The secret of my glowing health and no small part of my recent success." Mama and I hunkered down expectantly, knowing we were about to hear the story that was almost popping out of Pop.

"Back in April," he began, "I was on my way to Lubbock to talk to some people at Texas Tech about my wind-power idea—and frankly, I was feeling a little down, because I'd been spinning wheels for months without get- ting anywhere. But then I saw the sign!"

"The sign" sounded like some kind of vision from above. But when Pop stretched out a hand to mark the words, I realized he meant a highway billboard: "'YOUR DREAMS COME TRUE AT MOTOR MIKE'S! Now at two convenient locations! Come see our fabulous new RV Lot!' And listen to this: at that very minute, the *very minute* that billboard caught my attention, I heard Motor Mike himself on the radio, talking up his one-time-only grand-opening promotion. At that moment, I heard the knock of destiny." (My ears perked up—what did Kent Clark say about destiny?)

"I drove right over to Motor Mike's," Pop continued, "and signed up for his hard-body contest."

"His *what?*" Mama gasped. "You're in good shape for a man your age, Dad, but—"

"The body in question belonged to the prize," Pop said with a little frown. "Not the contestants." (I don't think he likes references to his age.) "I'd been thinking that the main problem with my new business was presentation. Here I was, driving an old pickup and living in that camper that Gee has such a low opinion of—" Pop broke off in alarm when Gee flung himself back on the floor and laughed like a maniac. Dropping his name in conversation is one of the things that sets him off, but I shushed him.

"Anyway," Pop went on, "by the time I got to Motor Mike's, there was only one contestant space left, and who got it? Yours truly."

I wasn't getting this. "But what *is* a hard-body contest?"

He held up his hand. "Picture this. Saturday morning, five-thirty a.m. A fiery pink-and-orange sunrise splashed over a big Texas sky. Rows of gleaming pickups and campers under strings of white lights. Motor Mike himself on a flatbed trailer with the mayor and state representatives and local deejay. The high school band. TV cameras and radio mikes. Fifty hopeful contestants in bright orange vests. And in the middle of the whole scene: bright, sparkling, in all its maroon-and-white glory, a brand-new Coachman RV."

"Hey!" Gee exclaimed. "Just like yours!"

I sighed, but Pop smiled gently. "Speeches are finally over. The band members finger their horns and woodwinds. A drumroll sounds. Motor Mike raises a pistol. Everybody sucks in a deep breath, and—*pow!* Fifty hands clamp to the body of that vehicle like magnets." He slapped a hand against his knee so suddenly we jumped. "This triumph of the automaker's art will go to the last man standing."

We sat absolutely still, even Gee, as his meaning sank in.

"But how did you go to the *bathroom*?" Gee burst out then.

Pop explained, and for once he didn't overdo it. Each contestant had to keep at least one hand flat on the vehicle at all times. They got fifteen-minute rest periods every six hours, and five-minute bathroom breaks every hour. Once in a while all the contestants would pick up their lawn chairs or camp stools and walk around the vehicle— never lifting their hands, of course—for ten minutes at a time. Otherwise, they just stood there, exchanging recipes and family news and friendly insults—which got less friendly as the minutes dragged by, slowly adding up to hours. The sun went down, the temperature dropped, and the audience dwindled to friends and relatives cheering on Mom or Uncle Steve or Linda Sue. The chilly predawn hours dragged in day two. Heavy clouds gathered to choke off the sunrise. At midmorning, they let loose with a Texas gully-washer that lasted an hour and left the contestants looking like drowned cats. Another day crept by, then another night. . . .

"They're a determined bunch," Pop said, "worthy opponents every one. But at the beginning of the third day, they're starting to drop off. Grandmas, plumbers, a marine, a mother of six—one by one they peel away. Hands that have to stay flat are starting to curl, like dry leaves in the fall. Every hour, another one staggers away or gets the disqualifying whistle. The sun sets again. During the night, eighteen more contestants hit the asphalt. I just pop my supplements and talk to stay awake. By the time it's all over, every contestant and car salesman and TV reporter in the lot will know my life story, philosophy, and long-term goals. Not to mention the equivalent of a college-level course in wind power.

"Day four dawns on about one-third the original number. By noon, five say adios. At sundown, three more collapse. During the fourth night, they drop like flies. At nine a.m. on the fifth day, I'm facing just one opponent, a feisty little one-hundred-ten-pound aircraft mechanic named Maria Garcia. The hours creep by. My hands are shaking, but hers shake worse. 'Ain't worth it, Maria,' I start telling her, even though my voice is almost shot by now. 'You've got a loving family and a boyfriend who's crazy about you and a fine life ahead—you don't need this vehicle. What you need is a real bed. A big puffy pillow. Your mama to rub your back and feet. . . .'

"There's a big crowd gathered because they know the end is near. Some of our former competition is cheering us on: 'Way to go, Jack!' 'Hang in there, Maria!' But her eyelids are heavy; her head starts to bob. As night creeps across the sky, her knees buckle—she's blacking out. A hush falls over the crowd. Her hand slides away from the passenger door, soft as a feather."

And that made John Q. Hazeltine (better known as Jack), after one hundred and nine hours, thirteen minutes, and seven seconds, the last man standing.

Mama looked absolutely mesmerized, and I was just *tingling*. Talk about meeting your short-term goals!

Gee finally broke the silence, whispering, "Wow."

After helping me clean up the kitchen and watching half an hour of TV—which he said was all he could stand—Pop went out to his double-size Royal Eaze mattress in the bunk of the RV (with the comfortable two feet of headroom). Mama managed to get to bed pretty much on her own with the help of rented crutches. I stuck a pillow under Gee where he'd fallen asleep on the living room floor and went to bed myself, thinking it had turned out to be one of the better days of my life. I fell asleep to the smooth, remembered sound of wheels rolling under my

reclining swivel seat, floating over the open road on steel-
spring suspension. . . .

But as good as Sunday ended, Monday opened up rainbows, sunbeams, and white-water rapids of potential goodness. Because right after I came out of the bathroom, before anybody else was up, Mama whispered from her bed, "Ronnie?"

I tiptoed in, expecting she needed help finding her crutches.

Instead, she murmured, "I've been thinking. When your grandfather heads out to Kansas in a few days, what if you and Gee went with him?"

3

Don't take No *for an answer.*

Turn your negatives into positives!

—Kent Clark,
Seize the Way

My first thought: *Wow, just what I was thinking!* Minus Gee, though. I couldn't see Pop consenting to a road trip with a hyperactive seven-year-old. But Kent Clark says to zap negative thoughts, so I took out my imaginary zapper and fired away while Mama explained that she wasn't exactly trying to get rid of us, but—

"The doctor told me the quickest way to recover would be complete and total rest—but the doctor doesn't know Gee, does he? Complete and total rest, my foot! Also, it would be a perfect opportunity for Lyddie and me to get a head start on the projects we want to sell at craft shows this fall. And the trip would be good for you, Ronnie. Because first, if you stay here you'll have almost all the responsibility of looking out for Gee, and that's no way to spend a summer vacation." (At this, I nodded so hard my neck hurt.) "Two, you'd get to know your grandfather better. Three, you'd get to see more of the country, even if it's just Kansas. Oh, and four, you'd get to take a trip in a real RV, instead of just mooning over the pictures and diagrams you bring home from the state fair."

Bottom line: her dream was to start her own craft business and mine was to take an RV trip. We'd kill two dreams with one stone. I was sold, but: "Do you think Pop'll go for it?"

She smiled and leaned back on the pillows. "He's not the only one with plans."

Her plan involved a big buildup. First, we'd learn all we could about Pop's wind-prospecting business. Second, figure out how I could help him in it. And finally, keep Gee under wraps as much as possible, because my little brother in full ADHD mode could scare off a saint. It was a big job, especially the last part. But we got a boost from the Partly Baptist Church, because their Vacation Bible School started that very morning.

We let Gee sleep in as late as possible, and right after breakfast I walked him to church. Even taking the long way, he was the first to arrive, not counting the teachers and their kids. I signed him up before anyone could have second thoughts, then rushed home to make myself obviously useful while listening in on conversations like this:

MAMA: So you're planning to travel all over western Kansas looking for the windiest spots to build power farms?

POP: That's it in a nutshell. Check for velocity, sustainability, shifts, and gusts. I find a spot and set up a meteorological mast—or met mast, as we say in the business—attach a weather vane on top and an anemometer to do the measuring, then I go back and check on it for three or four days. What that does . . . [explain, explain]

MAMA: (after the explaining is over) And how do you keep track of all that information?

POP: Ah. The university is supposed to give me a

laptop to run the data, but I hate trying to figure out computer programs. Not looking forward to that.

MAMA: By the way, did I show you Ronnie's last report card? All As in math, and her teacher told me she's at the top of her class in computer skills. . . .

That's me—world-class record-keeper and number-cruncher. Plus, I'm very neat and systematic—Exacto-girl. "Hey, Pop, I'm organizing my room. Come see what I plan to do with my closet!"

After Vacation Bible School, my job was to keep Gee away from Pop so it wouldn't be so obvious what a challenge he presented. Gee spent most of the afternoon with neighborhood kids, but it was exhausting to be on full radar alert. Tuesday was better—that is, until the end.

Tuesday morning I finished cleaning up Mama's bedroom while Pop fixed the leaky faucet in the kitchen and replaced the torn screen on the storm door. After lunch, he dropped Gee and me off at the Polk County Library and went on down to Springfield to shop for his Kansas expedition. While Gee interrupted story hour with goofy questions, I found some books on alternative power and meteorology. Then we walked to the pool, and even though Pop picked us up later than he said he would, I was sweet as cherry pie all the way home. And made sure he saw me reading my books. I even thought of some questions to ask him and listened all the way through his explanations.

While washing up after dinner (which I cooked), I heard him say, "That Ronnie . . . she's pretty sharp. I never thought a twelve-year-old kid could be so interested in weather."

"Sometimes she reminds me of you, Dad," my mother replied. "She has goals and ambitions coming out the wazoo. You know what she wanted for her birthday? Her very own business cards."

"No kidding?" Pop sounded impressed. "How many kids would think of that?"

Not many—all my friends at school just said "What's this for?" when I handed out business cards. Like they thought I should have a business or something. Plus, we moved four months later so the address and phone numbers are no good. I crossed out the old info and printed the new by hand, but it looks dorky.

"She wants to buy her own car *before* she can legally drive."

"Huh. So did I."

"Really? So, did you?" Mom's voice took on that teasing tone she uses to keep a good mood going.

"Not exactly. . . . Gee's still a handful, isn't he?"

"Now, he's a sweet boy at heart. But sometimes he needs a firm hand, and at the end of a long day I'm just exhausted. He could sure use a father figure. You're a real good influence on him, Dad—I can see it."

"Well . . . ," Pop said thoughtfully. "I do what I can."

It sounded to me like he was softening up. I gave the knives and forks one last rattle under the rinse water and dropped them in the drainer, just in time to hear my mother finish asking, ". . . take them with you for the next week or so?"

Of course I didn't expect him to say "Hey, that's a great

idea!" But what he said surprised me anyway: "*What?!* Are you crazy?"

Did you ever, as a little kid, start down a really high slide and find yourself going a whole lot faster than you expected? Like it just rained or somebody spilled their French fries on it? That's how I felt, zooming down a slide of negativity. Toward the bottom I was trying to slow myself down, whispering, *Don't take no for an answer, don't take no for an answer, don't take no—*

But *no* is what I kept hearing from the next room.

MAMA: All I ask is that you live up to your responsibility for a change!

POP: What responsibility? They're *your* kids!

MAMA: But I'm *your* kid! I always will be, even though you left when I was thirteen—

POP: Wait a minute. Are you saying it's my fault you're stuck in the middle of Missouri with a couple of kids and a bad knee?

MAMA: Of *course* not! But you're my *father.* Is it too much to expect that you'll be around for me when I need your help?

POP: Where've I been these last three days?

MAMA: Three days once a year—but who's counting? I'm only asking for one or two weeks out of your whole life. And you're not even going that far away! Kansas is right next door. If it doesn't work out you can bring them back anytime—

POP: I'd lose a whole day or more on the job if I did that—

MAMA: What's more important, a job or a human being? These children need you! Just like I did. . . .

She'd been speaking real firm up to then, with lots of exclamation marks. But all of a sudden her voice choked up and turned weepy: "You could make some effort to pay back . . . a little of what you took away—"

I peeked around the doorframe. Mama, from her nest of pillows on the sofa, was reaching for a Kleenex. Pop was sitting upright in the recliner, both hands clutching the chair arms. What surprised me was his expression: not angry but desperate, like a cornered fox.

What to do now? My brain was shuffling through ideas when Gee sealed the deal by falling off the top of the RV.

Of course, none of us knew he was even *on* the RV until we heard shouts from the front yard. I know Gee's hurt-screams from his scared-screams, but this was both. Mama jumped up, suddenly remembered her knee, and fell back on the pillows with a gasp of pain. I shot out of the kitchen and through the living room. When I reached the front porch, Pop was right behind me.

What happened was, Gee had tied on his Superman cape (a red towel with a ribbon sewn to it) and gathered some of the neighborhood kids to watch him fly. After climbing to the RV's sundeck, he aimed for an old baby-crib mattress he'd dragged out from the garage. But after Gee's hyperactive-baby abuse, that mattress wasn't up to much. It broke the fall, but only a little more gently than bare concrete. Casey and Judy Lavender were screaming right along with Gee, and Hunter Rice was on his way up the ladder to try it himself.

I went for Gee; Pop went for Hunter, grabbing him firmly by the belt and setting him on the driveway with a shake. The other kids took off like roaches when you turn the light on. Gee howled all the time I was checking him for broken bones, but stopped when our grandfather knelt down and gave him a look like a hammer gives a nail.

I tried to save the situation. "You shouldn't have been up there without asking Pop's permission." But even in my sternest voice, it sounded lame. Pop felt Gee over with his lips tucked in tight, and once we were both satisfied that he wasn't hurt—beyond the skinned elbow that missed the mattress—I helped him up and took him to Mama's open arms.

Gee burrowed in beside her while I watched her pillowcases get all smeary with blood. Who was going to have to wash them? Me. Mama knew her plan had just gone down the garbage disposal but couldn't quite let it go. She looked up at Pop, who had come in behind me, and sniffed, "All he needs is a firm hand."

About an hour later, after muttering something about how fish and visitors stink after three days, Pop backed his new RV out of the drive and rolled away.

Mama sighed. "It seemed like a good idea at the time."

Gee's only penalty was going to bed early. Since he sort of sacks out wherever in our two-bedroom house, that meant exile in Mama's room, where he scattered her button collection to make a minefield of her bed.

Meanwhile, I shut myself in my room and opened my journal to where I'd written *Short-term Goals for Kan. Trip:*

1. Learn to organize better by living in RV.
2. Study Pop's biz style and method—mentor material?
3. See new places.
4. Get away from old places!

I ripped that page out, wadded it into a ball, and threw it across the room. You never know how much you wanted something until it's jerked away. I'd caught it like a fever: the open road and the rolling wheels and the big blue sky. I wanted to pack up and take myself places where everything I saw would fit somewhere inside me, like all that kitchenware and bedding and little comforts of home squared away inside the RV. Instead, I was looking at a summer that sprawled like Mama's wardrobe, with all the drawers hanging open and clothes spilled. Hello, square one.

On Wednesday, I walked Gee to Vacation Bible School, where his teacher still acted like she was glad to see him. Last year he was kicked out of a VBS in midweek for building a fort out of hymnbooks—which wouldn't have been so bad except that he glued them together. This year all he'd done—so far—was sneak out of class and dive into the baptistery.

Back home, I helped Mama set up a craft center in the living room. That is, I moved furniture and toted boxes while she changed her mind about where she wanted everything. It was a project I could have got interested in, if I hadn't been working so hard to climb out of my negativity pit.

When things were arranged so that Mama could reach supplies on one side and food and drink on the other, while propping up her bad knee and glancing at the TV, it was time to collect Gee at church.

His teacher met me with a serious look and drew me aside—always a bad sign. "We dealt with this already, but you should tell your mother that Gee bit one of his classmates today."

"Oh," I said.

"I used to teach the preschoolers, and they're all little biters, but by second grade they've usually grown out of it."

Before I could say "Oh" again, she rushed on. "Also, he has a real hard time paying attention. Has your mother looked into that?"

I assured her we'd been looking into that, and she gave Gee an extra-bright smile when saying good-bye to him. "So what's up with the biting?" I asked after we'd walked a block and turned a corner.

Gee, in a sulky mood, kicked a rock. "It's what that dopey-head Travis called me."

"What did he call you?"

"A dopey-head."

"Hmm." Gee gets a lot of that kind of thing. Not that he's stupid, but he has trouble reading because his eyes skip all over the page, and some of the questions and answers he blurts out in class are way beside the point. He also has anger issues, as dopey-head Travis found out. "Well, next time—"

"Look! A rabbit!"

He took off chasing the bunny, which darted into a culvert. That would have stopped most kids, but not Gee. I barely caught him before he disappeared for good, but not before he got pretty well slimed. "Yuck! When we get home, you've got a date with the garden hose!"

I'd better say this up front: I love my little brother, but it's tough sometimes not to see him as a big negative. Since reading Mr. Clark's book, I've tried to change my thinking. For instance, Gee loves to climb things, so last fall I started a little gutter-cleaning service in our neighborhood in Lee's Summit. I went door-to-door with my business cards one Saturday morning, telling people my brother would scrape the gutters while I cleaned up the soggy leaves and twigs that fell under the eaves. Five customers signed up, mostly elderly people and couples who worked during the day. I didn't mention to them that my brother was only six at the time. In fact, I might have left the impression he was closer to sixteen.

It worked just fine—we'd done three houses at twenty dollars each and Gee wasn't burned-out yet. Then I contracted a two-story house. Gee climbed up like a monkey, but once he was up there he freaked out and I had to call the fire department. Actually, the fire department in Lee's Summit already knew us pretty well.

"Ronnie?" Gee asked now, after a moment of silence.

"Huh?"

"Did I screw things up again?"

"What do you mean, screw things up? Don't wipe your face with your T-shirt! It's all green!"

"Is Pop not taking us to Kansas because I jumped off his camper?"

"It's not a camper, it's a— How'd you know about the Kansas idea?"

He just shrugged.

"Well," I said, "it probably wouldn't have flown anyway. He never stays with us for more than three days. It was probably crazy to think he'd want us for a whole week or more." I really meant "you," not "us," but was trying to be nice about the whole thing.

"You coulda gone. I'd stay here and take care of Mama."

I'll bet you would, I thought. But it was a sweet offer anyway. After a minute, I gave him a careful, sideways hug. "Thanks." We turned the corner onto our street. "But it would be good if you'd start using your head a little before—"

"Look!" he yelled, pointing toward our house.

I looked, blinked, still couldn't believe my eyes.

There in the driveway—high, wide, and shiny in the noonday sun—stood Pop's maroon-and-white RV.

CHAPTER
4

Every downside has an upside.

—Kent Clark,
Seize the Way

What changed his mind? He didn't say, and I didn't ask him.

Because the sight of that maroon-and-white house-on-wheels in our driveway again was like the test that got postponed. The eight ball that rolled into the corner pocket. The Screamin' Eagle at Six Flags that has room for one more rider, and I'm it. When your luck changes, don't ask why.

Pop was in the living room, perched on the very edge of the recliner as though unwilling to stay a minute longer than he had to. Mama was stomping around the bedroom on her crutches, scrounging clean underwear out of the laundry basket and stuffing it into an old gym bag. "Gee!" she exclaimed at the sight of him. "What did you do, crawl through a culvert? You've got two minutes to take a shower!"

"What's up?" I whispered.

Mama raised her shoulders, then her eyebrows. "He changed his mind. If you still want to, you can go. But listen to me, Ronnie. He told me that some days he'll be gone for hours at a time on his motorcycle and he'll have to leave you and Gee at a campground. I told him you're used to being in charge, but at home you have some backup, at least. It's an awful lot of responsibility. If you don't feel up to this—"

A week or more in an RV? "I'm *on* it."

"I know you are, sweetie. Just hope this isn't a big mistake. Have you seen Gee's inhaler?"

"Inhaler?!" Pop yelled from the living room. "What's that for?"

Mama's laugh sounded nervous. No wonder: a hyper little boy was one thing, but a hyper little boy who sometimes stopped breathing might send that RV out of the driveway even faster than the first time. "For his asthma, Dad. It's not serious. He just has a minor incident every few months—less all the time, really—and when it happens we all know what to do. Oh, and Ronnie—"

She signaled me to come closer, murmuring, "Be sure you take the Ritalin prescription. Just in case." She smiled really big, only it wasn't her usual smile. "One more thing—I bought a new cartridge for his Game Boy last month—Mad Mechanix. It's on the top shelf of the linen closet. Supposed to be a birthday present, but . . ."

She wiggled her fingers and I thought, *Good plan.* A new game could keep him occupied for most of our first day on the road, and part of the second, and maybe as much as an hour on the third, and by then we'd be so far away Pop would have to think twice about turning around to bring us home.

After his two-minute shower, which didn't quite get all the green off, Gee stuffed some action figures and a toothbrush in the gym bag Mama had packed for him. Then she sent him outside for a farewell tour of the neighborhood so he'd be out of our hair while I packed my own stuff. Mama hobbled back to the couch, where she kept remembering things to do: "Take some macaroni and cheese!" "See if I've got a calling card in my purse—and do you want to pack my old binoculars? I'm not sure where they are." "I need my glue gun! I think it's under the bed. . . ."

"All packed," I announced, marching through the living room with my duffel bag under one arm. "Where should I put this, Pop?" He only shrugged—a little stunned, I guess.

Mama was back on her feet, rummaging around in her desk drawer. As I went out the door, she called, "Bring your brother with you when you come back in."

Gee was in the driveway, trying to explain Pop's job to the neighborhood kids. In Gee-speak this came out as "wind prowler."

"What's that?" Casey wanted to know.

"He goes looking for wind," Gee said, "and we're gonna help."

"Help *how*? Wind just happens, whether you're looking or not."

I walked between them to get to the RV door, which is near the back and opens into the kitchen. The sink was directly ahead, dinette to the right, bathroom to the left. Everything was in its place, from the row of vitamin bottles above the sink to the row of books beside the bunk— not a stray spoon or sock or spatula. What I like about RVs is how efficient they are, every bit of space accounted for. Then it hit me: wherever I put my bag, it wouldn't belong. And *anywhere* Gee put himself, he didn't belong. He sure couldn't be tucked away like a spatula in his own special drawer.

No, the minute he came on board, this tidy little world would be wrecked. If my shy little duffel bag spoiled the order, just imagine what a mini-whirlwind could do. Maybe this trip wasn't such a good idea.

I shook my head and tried to think like Kent Clark: when you come to a fork in the road, take it! Or something like that. I dropped my bag on the nearest dinette seat.

Pop came out of the house and the bon voyage committee scattered at the sight of him. "Go on and say goodbye to your mother," he said to Gee and me. We started in, but his next words stopped us: "I told her that I had work to do, and if you kids give me any trouble, we'll turn around and come right back here, understand?"

"Yes, sir," I said, nodding fiercely at Gee.

"Yes, sir," he repeated.

In the house I got a long hug from Mama, who said, "Honey, I sure hope this works out. If you start having doubts, let me know and I'll ask him to bring you back. Or send Lyddie if he can't. Here's my calling card—sure wish your grandfather had a cell phone, but he's been too stubborn to get one. So watch for pay phones, and let me hear from me, okay?"

"Okay."

"Try to help your grandfather, and keep Gee out of trouble, and have a good time. Not necessarily in that order, though. Love you."

"Love you, too."

"And one more thing." She gave me an envelope. "I put a few dollars and some stamps in here. I want you to buy postcards and make Gee write to me every day. Or have him tell you what he wants to say while you write it down, and make sure he stays on topic. More or less. His teacher told me that writing or dictating will help him focus. One more thing for you to worry about, but—"

"I'll do it, Mama."

After a final hug, I let Gee at her. She told him the usual stuff about being good and minding me and Pop, even though she knew he'd forget it as soon as we backed out of the driveway. Then she wiped her eyes and told him to go to the bathroom one more time.

Gee took the dinette seat, facing forward, with his lunch-box full of Roman gladiators and race cars on the table in front of him. Once he was buckled in, he froze up. It had finally dawned on him that he really was leaving his home and Mama for a long time. One of his therapists explained that in different situations he might pull into himself, like a turtle, in order to size up his new environment and decide where he fit. He'd be busting out of himself soon enough, I figured. So it was time to size up my own new environment and decide where I fit while I still had the chance.

Kent Clark says the best way to do that is to listen, which means get the other guy talking. Once we were on the highway, I said, "I've been reading up on wind power. Do you really think it has a future?"

Questions like that pushed Pop's explaining button, and he went on for quite a while. I had already heard most of it, but then he added, "The thing about wind power is, you can't make it. Can't tell the wind where or when to blow, or how hard. But you can learn to work with it. Kind of like rowing the flow."

I sat up straighter, all ears. "Right! I get it. So what's the plan? Like, what's our first stop?"

"The university in Pittsburg, Kansas. I've got an appointment in the morning with a couple of professors in the physics department. They got hold of a government grant—"

"You mean money?" I interrupted.

"Yeah, salary and expenses. Not that expenses are much—all I need are a few instruments for measuring wind on the plains and the gas to get me out there."

His overall plan was to park the RV in campgrounds for three or four days at a time and set up temporary wind-tracking stations at various spots within a sixty-mile radius. He'd visit each spot every day on his Yamaha. "Then," he went on, "I record all the data and run averages. They're giving me a wireless laptop for that, but I don't look forward to figuring out the program."

Bingo! "I can do that."

He glanced over at me. "You can?"

"Sure. You saw my report card—all As in computer skills."

"Oh. Right." The wheels started turning in his head. I snuck a glance and a thumbs-up sign at Gee. He was looking at trees and hills outside his window and shifted his gaze to me with no change of expression, like I was another tree.

"Heads up, kids," Pop announced. "We just crossed the border into Kansas."

I faced forward in time to see the WELCOME billboard flash by. Kansas looked just like Missouri. It still did about half an hour later when we pulled into a campground, where Gee finally let loose. Since it was a little RV park with not much to do, "letting loose" meant running around the loop a few times, splashing in the creek nearby, and picking up a dozen ticks in the woods. For dinner we had chicken noodle soup and canned green beans. "I'm not much of a cook," Pop said while cranking the can opener. "When we get to a grocery store tomorrow, you kiddos can pick out what you like."

Bingo! I thought again. Cooking is not my favorite thing, but I can do meat loaf, baked potatoes, mushroom soup chicken, and Casserole à la Sparks. If we stopped at a used-book store long enough for me to get my hands on a cookbook, I could add to my repertoire.

When I suggested this, Pop's expression brightened, like he was thinking the grandparent gig might not be so tough after all. Then I volunteered to wash up and he offered to take Gee to the creek and show him how to hunt crawdads. They walked down the path as sweet as a Hallmark card, and I had the place to myself for a while. I looked around to see what needed organizing.

We hadn't messed up anything too much yet. The interior still looked like a picture on one of those brochures I used to pick up, where there's an open coloring book on the table or a sliced onion on the kitchen counter to show that the place can actually be lived in. I didn't leave the dishes in the itty-bitty sink to drain, but dried them and put them away in their proper stacks in the cabinet. Then I squeezed out the dishcloth and laid it over the edge of the sink. But that didn't look right, so I draped it over the neck of the faucet—any better? A towel rod under the sink would be best, and I was looking for a place to mount one when Gee's unmistakable scream dropped on me like a bomb.

I was streaking down the path toward the creek even before the echoes had died away. A little crowd had gathered on the bank—two men, one woman, and a girl about Gee's age—all trying to make him stop jumping up and down and spinning in circles while he yelled, "Ow! Ow! Ow!" Pop stood a little ways off, shaking his head.

"What happened?" I panted.

"The craziest thing. I caught a crawdad for him so he could see it up close. He wants to hold it, so I let him, and then . . . he kisses it. So what's a self-respecting crawdad supposed to do?"

I could see it now—about three inches long with a little lobster-like tail and one waving claw. The other claw was the part attached to Gee's chin. "Little boy," the woman kept insisting, "you have to hold *still*." She finally clamped him down by the shoulders, and while Gee paddled the air, whimpering, one of the guys pulled the critter loose.

"Eeeeuw," said the girl.

"Why would he do something like that?" Pop murmured to me.

"Scientific curiosity?" I suggested.

Gee did show some curiosity once the crustacean let go of him—in fact, he wanted to keep it for a pet. But the man who'd pulled it off his chin said their chances for bonding were shot. After thanking him, Pop told us, "I'm going back to the truck. Gee, why don't you show your sister how to find crawdads?"

Which I took to mean, *You kiddos stay out of my hair for a while.* Obviously, I would be spending a lot of this kind of quality time with my brother. It was kind of fun, though, turning over the flat rocks to see if there were any gray fantailed critters underneath. Gee was *trying* to get bit now, but the crawdads had their little minds set on escape.

When it got too dark to see them, we went back to our campsite. Pop sent us to the camp shower—a disappointment to Gee, who wanted to take an itty-bitty shower in the RV. But the long day and the crustacean experience had settled him down, and he was mostly quiet and polite about it. Also about getting his jammies on while I made up the sofa (for me) and the dinette seat (for him). And sometime during the night, he quietly and politely wet the bed.

He's almost stopped doing that, but sometimes slips up in a new environment, or when he's upset or worried or scared. At first, I forgot about turning my negatives into positives. "How *could* you?" I hissed at him, gathering up the sheet before Pop could see it. "Now I have to figure out some way to do laundry." Gee stuck his thumb in his mouth, which he hasn't done for years.

Kent Clark says not to major in minors—meaning don't freak out over details. Pulling out Gee's thumb, I said, "It'll be okay. Better than okay—once you get used to traveling, it'll be fun. You'll just have to . . . you know, practice thinking before you kiss crawdads or scream or . . ." I wasn't sure how he'd practice not wetting the bed. "Anyway, you'll do better next time, right?"

I stuffed the sheet in one of the RV's outside compartments and sponged off the dinette mattress. Then I found eggs and bacon in the fridge and cooked them up to order (scrambled, a little on the wet side; bacon crisp). Pop was in a good mood when we hit the road.

Gee was feeling good, too, after crunching down four slices of bacon—but a lot more fidgety than the day before. After only fifteen minutes, he was unbuckling his seat belt for the least little reason, like to straighten the pockets on his jeans. Pop was feeling talky, so while one side of me was listening to him explain all his vitamin and mineral supplements and why he took them, the other side was making signals and frowny faces at the backseat.

Fortunately, we didn't have far to go—less than an hour. Gee had taken the laces out of his shoes and was making a noose when Pop steered into a shady parking lot in front of a red-brick building. ". . . so the chelation cleans all the metals out of my system," Pop was explaining. "You'll have to listen to that tape sometime, Ronnie. You wouldn't believe all the heavy metal that's floating around in your body."

"Wow," I replied, making a lunge for Gee, who'd just stuck his head in the noose and pulled it, making his eyes cross and his tongue poke out. No telling what was floating around in his body.

Pop reached behind the seat for his hat and a briefcase. "This is the science building," he told us. "The meeting will probably last an hour or so, so why don't y'all . . . take a walk. Be good."

I waited until he was almost out of sight before letting my brother loose, and Gee barreled down the sidewalk so fast he almost knocked over a lady with a baby stroller. "Sorry," I gasped while chasing after him. I'd almost caught up when we turned a corner and ran smack into a glorious sight: a fountain splashing in a shady plaza. An inspiration flashed in my brain that would have made Kent Clark proud. Every downside has an upside!

Gee attacked the fountain the way he sometimes attacks playground equipment (I've seen smaller kids flee in terror). Catching him just before he took the plunge, I said, "Hold it! We've got something to do first."

Back at the RV, I pulled the damp sheet from the storage compartment and poured a little detergent into a jar. "We're going to use the fountain as a washing machine. You can be the agitator."

"What's that?"

"That thing in the machine that stirs up the water."

"Cool!"

In the fountain he tried out at least a dozen agitator moves, but what worked best was jumping up and down while the white sheet billowed under his feet like a cloud. The detergent was a little sudsier than I expected and got us more attention from passersby than I was looking for, but otherwise it worked great. Gee went snorkeling (as he called it) while I wrung out the laundry and spread it over a bush to dry. That also worked until a passing dog took off with it. The upside of *that* was giving Gee something else to do, namely chase the dog around the fountain while I rinsed the dirtiest corner of the sheet. This day was showing more upsides than a skillet full of pancakes.

When Pop found us, we were sitting on a bench near the RV with a dampish bedsheet spread out behind us. He didn't appear to notice it. He'd had a good morning, too; there was a spring in his step and a new laptop tucked under his arm. "Head 'em up and move 'em out!" he said. "We're on our way!"

CHAPTER

5

Periodically, try to step back and
take a look at the big picture.

—Kent Clark,
Oh, you know the name of the book by now.

Back in the RV, I gave Gee an orange to peel, along with his lunchbox of cars and gladiators. If we were lucky, we might get through another day without breaking out Mad Mechanix. When he'd eaten half the orange, he made a slingshot out of a rubber band and used it to shoot seeds and bits of peel at his gladiators. Little "pow"s and "bam"s came from the dinette as we left Pittsburg, heading west.

Pop chuckled in a grandfatherly manner. "I wish he'd sell me some of that energy."

Actually, I've often wished I could sell Gee's energy. "Do you think it's possible to use kid-power somehow? Like with a treadmill?"

That earned another chuckle. "If power could be generated that way, I'd be making a fortune in hamsters. In the old days, treadmills were used to turn fireplace spits and simple machines, but we've moved way beyond that now. If you had ten little brothers like Gee, that could add up to something."

"Uh-huh," I said, "my funeral."

Pop laughed out loud—he sure was feeling good. "Hear that, Gee?" At the moment, my brother was playing demolition-derby-in-the-Colosseum, and didn't hear it.

"You know," Pop went on, "he just seems like a normal boy to me. Sure, he gets a little out of hand sometimes, but I don't think it's anything some old-fashioned discipline can't fix. I could tell you stories about myself at that age. . . ."

I glanced back in time to see Gee aiming a matchbox car at us with a rubber band, which made me lunge toward him and slash a finger across my throat. He knows what that means.

"Before we head out west," Pop said, "let's be tourists. There's a sight I want to see a little ways south of here."

Up till now, I'd thought that "tourists" went to see sights like Buckingham Palace and the pyramids. "What is it, Pop?"

"A shovel."

He grinned, so I knew there was more to it. There *had* to be more to it. "Cool! Is it very far?"

"About an hour and a half. You want to rustle up some sandwiches for us?"

That gave me something to do—and Gee, too, since I usually let him make his own sandwich. The rule is, if he makes it, he has to eat it, even if it's peanut butter and ketchup with bananas. The whole lunch thing took about forty minutes, after which Gee settled down with his eyelids at half-mast. That left me free to watch the scenery.

While Pop was explaining to me how the medical establishment was in cahoots with the drug companies, I began to notice Kansas looking less like Missouri. The roads were straighter, like they'd been drawn with a ruler. They went on longer, too. We drove due west for miles and miles, then made a sharp left to go south. I lost count of how many sharp turns we made until I started seeing signs that pointed the way to "Big Brutus." "What's that?" I asked.

"That's our destination," he said with another grin.

Thinking this might be better than it had sounded at first, I looked back at Gee, who was beginning to stir out of sleep mode. "Did you hear that? We're going to see a shovel named Big Brutus!"

He blinked a couple of times. "A big shovel? You mean like Mike Mulligan?"

"Right!" Mike Mulligan's steam shovel was so far back—like in kindergarten—I'd forgotten about that happy-jawed hunk of iron crunching up rock. But I was glad to be reminded. Now I had some idea what to expect.

Except I didn't.

First of all, this thing is out in the middle of *no*where. We're driving by open fields and little towns with water towers, wondering how much farther, and then all of a sudden it's THERE, rearing up behind a row of rooftops. It's an orange-backed monster with one huge black arm reaching up ("That's the boom," said Pop) and another one reaching down ("That's the dipper stick—it operates the shovel part"). The whole machine just kind of jumped up against the sky, so sudden I was speechless for a minute. But that's nothing: so was Gee.

More turns, more straight roads and gulpy views, until finally we pulled into a parking lot facing an open field, with a pond and a visitor center—and Big Brutus himself, in all his jaw-droppingness, tall as a skyscraper way out here on the Kansas plains. Pop grabbed his camera.

Gee couldn't wait to get at it, even though the machine looked like it could eat him alive and not even burp. But Pop is the type who likes to "orient" himself, meaning at least half an hour in the visitor center looking over the exhibits and letting us know what he learned. "Hey, kids! It says the bucket holds ninety cubic yards!" "Listen to this: the body of the steam shovel is sixteen stories high!" Meanwhile, I was chasing Gee from window to window and blocking doors to keep him in.

The postcard rack distracted him for a while; he couldn't decide which card to send to Mama first. His favorite was the one with a cowboy sitting on a giant jackrabbit over the caption *Herding Cattle in Kansas*, but I told him we should send pictures of things we were really seeing. "And jackrabbits don't grow that big here—or any-where."

He rolled his eyes. "I *know* that. But it's funny, and Mama could use a laugh."

I sometimes forget—he's weird, but he's not stupid. So I agreed to the jackrabbit, and since cards were three for a dollar we each picked one with Brutus on it. To kill more time while Pop was chatting up the salesclerk, I dragged Gee over to the brochure rack. "Look—here's all the cool stuff in Kansas we might be able to see. Rock City, Wizard of Oz Museum, World's Largest Hand-Dug Well. Or how about the World's Largest Ball of Twine . . . ?"

"What's this?" He pounced on a card at one end of a row. The full-color picture on the front showed a man in a silvery outfit with a golden helmet under one arm. That's all I could tell with Gee waving the card in front of my face. "It says *Human Cannon!*"

"Hold still." I snatched the card out of his hand and read, *The Blazing, Amazing Cannonball Paul! Limited Engagement! See back for dates and locations.*

"But what is it?" Gee demanded. "What's a Human Cannon?"

"Cannon*ball*. It's a guy who goes around getting himself shot out of a gun." I pointed to the huge rifle-barrel thing behind the man.

My brother's eyes went big and round. "You mean over and over? Like, he never gets killed?"

"Of course he doesn't get killed. He knows how to do it." As a career choice, though, it was definitely weird.

Our grandfather called, "Y'all ready to see Big Brutus?"

"Pop!" Gee grabbed the card from my hand and bounded over. "We've gotta see this guy!"

"What's that?" Pop glanced at the front of the card, then turned to the schedule of dates on the back. "Maybe. If we're in one of these places at the right time."

That wasn't good enough for Gee, who kept pestering him all the way out of the visitor center.

I stayed behind to pay for the postcards, while the clerk gushed at me, "You kids are going to have a great time seeing Kansas—you're lucky to have such a nice grandfather!"

That must have been some impression he made on her. She looked like a sensible lady, aside from a heavy hand with the mascara. I couldn't stay to talk, though; Gee might at that very moment be driving our nice grandfather to distraction.

I'd learned from the visitor-center exhibits that Brutus was built right where it stands (being too big to move). There used to be a lot of coal here, and Brutus's job was to remove the rock and dirt on top of the coal so smaller shovels could get at it. Once the coal was gone, Brutus didn't have anything to do. Instead of scrapping it, the mining company donated the shovel and the land it was on to some local organization that fixed it up for tours.

Pop sure did like a tour. He stopped at every single site listed in the self-guiding brochure and read the explanation out loud. Stop number one was the bucket, or "dipper, which held ninety cubic yards or approximately one hundred forty tons of material." Area-wise, the dipper was as big as our living room and almost twice as high.

Gee was acting sulky—he and Pop had probably had words about Cannonball Paul—so he refused to stand with me in the dipper to have our picture taken. But the iron teeth that stuck out from the lower jaw might have spooked him a little; in fact, now that he was up close and personal with this humongous thing, he seemed subdued—as if its sheer size had packed him into a ball of subduedness.

Once we were *inside* the humongous thing, though, he started expanding again. Inside Big Brutus is an ADHD fun house: rollers, gears, cables, ladders, and lots of portholes labeled KEEP OUT.

I don't know if "porthole" is the right word, but they were definitely holes, about four feet long, built into the metal walls. Pop said they led to the guts of the machine, where crewmen used to crawl around oiling parts. Of course Gee disappeared into one the minute my back was turned, and when I started looking for him he popped out: "Pow! I'm a human cannonball!"

I grabbed him by the sleeve and pointed to the wall. "Look what it says: KEEP OUT. Two words. Which one do you not understand?"

"Hey!" Pop called from station eighteen. "Listen to this: 'The main hoist was operated by eight five-hundred-horsepower DC electric motors. There are eight hundred feet of cable on each side. . . .' "

All those numbers started to mean something when we got to the boom. There's a narrow door beside the operator's cab that lets you go right out on it. Then you can climb 150 feet of steps to the observation platform at the top.

I was dying to climb those steps, but first we had to discuss my age, because nobody under thirteen was allowed on the boom. I was almost thirteen—just four more months. Pop suggested talking to the gift-store lady for special permission, and I had to wonder if he wanted to gaze into her heavy-duty mascara again. But it was a long walk back to the gift shop, so he decided to let me fudge a little. First I would watch Gee (who'd never pass for thirteen) while Pop finished the self-guided tour in peace, and then we would switch off.

Easier said than done, of course—try keeping a hyper seven-year-old occupied in a big machine full of ladders and I-beams and holes that say KEEP OUT. To make it worse, a couple of teenage boys with floppy tank tops joined us and set a bad example by ducking in and out of the holes themselves.

Finally, Pop returned to take charge of Gee, and when I got my chance to climb to the top of those 150 steps, it was worth the effort. I could see all the way to Missouri, or it sure seemed like it. Kent Clark talks about stepping back to look at the big picture, and if that wasn't a big picture I don't know what is: miles and miles of land rolled out in every direction like a huge gray-green quilt marked with roads, dotted with houses and little towns, stitched up with tiny tractors. It all looked so normal—except for the fact that I was seeing it from the boom of a sixteen-story electric shovel out in the middle of nowhere. I looked with one eye, then the other, then with both eyes a little squinty, wondering if there was some kind of inspiration to be had from this particular big picture.

Then I heard my name, out of the blue: "RONNIIIIIE!" Not a voice from the sky, but you probably already guessed that. The likely scenario was that Gee had slipped away from Pop—who didn't yet understand what "watching him" meant—and pushed through the narrow door leading to the boom. I turned around, expecting to see him clutching the guardrails halfway up. But the steps were empty. And the noise was still going on.

When I finally spotted him, it felt like the air had made a fist and punched me in the chest. There he was, a little boy in a red T-shirt, clinging to an I-beam jutting out from the metal wall, about fifteen stories off the ground. The only way he could have got there was by shinnying up the support post rising from the platform, just outside the door. He'd had to climb almost six feet to reach the horizontal beam, which he'd wrapped himself around before looking down. Then he panicked, having set a personal best for not-looking-prior-to-leaping.

And by now he had a lot more attention than just mine. An older couple and a dad with two kids were staring up from the ground, pointing or wringing their hands. One of the teenage boys came out on the stair landing and yelled, "DUDE!" Pop squeezed by and staggered in shock when he saw where Gee was. I pounded down the stairs to meet him, and we had a little discussion.

POP: What the @#$! is wrong with this kid?

ME: Gee, stop screaming! And don't look down.

TEENAGE BOY: (through the door) Dude! Hey, Brad! Come look at this!

Pop is a man of action, but climbing poles umpteen dozen feet off the ground is not exactly his kind of action. He tried to reach Gee by hoisting himself up on the platform railings, but when he put one foot up and tried to raise the other, his face turned the color of biscuit dough and he broke out in a sweat.

"Hey, man. Let me give it a shot." The other boy, Brad, had ducked through the little door. Brad was about six and a half feet tall, which turned out to be very useful in a situation like this. He stepped up on the railings, balancing his weight between them, and when he stood up straight his head was level with Gee's. "Hey, little buddy, how's it goin'?"

I wanted to say, *Hold on tight, Gee!* But of course he was already holding so tight he was frozen. Brad had to reassure him about a dozen times before Gee loosened up enough to let go of the I-beam, edge around the vertical pole, and clamp on to the tall guy's shoulders. Brad carefully stepped back down onto the platform and delivered him safely into my arms.

We didn't stick around. After shaking Brad's hand, Pop hustled us down to the parking lot without even stopping in to say good-bye to the gift-shop lady.

I thought he might explode when we got to the RV, like Mama does sometimes: *Don't you* ever *scare me like that again!* But his color still wasn't quite right, so maybe he just wanted to forget the whole thing as soon as possible. I took over the parent part while checking Gee's seat belt: "What were you *thinking?*"

He stuck his thumb in his mouth. I knew the answer anyway—once he'd got out on that platform, all those pipes and rails overwhelmed his reasoning power. "One good thing," I told Pop while moving up to my own seat, "every time he does something like that, it puts the fear of God into him for at least a week." I couldn't tell if Pop was especially reassured, but when we got back to the highway we were still headed west.

A couple hours of driving got us to a campground southwest of Wichita that happened to have a pool and a Jacuzzi. Everybody felt better after their preferred water therapy. Pop may even have harbored a little guilt for failing to rescue Gee when he had the chance—whatever the reason, he played Grandpa to the hilt that night. After I helped Gee to write his first postcard, Pop even sat down to play Go Fish with us, but after two rounds he said, "Let's play a *real* card game."

Then he taught us poker: five-card draw and seven-card stud, with matchsticks for money.

Poker is a *lot* more fun than Go Fish, let me tell you—especially if you win a few hands. Gee didn't win any, but a couple of times he thought he had. The first time he upset his soda can, and the second time he knocked the dinette table off its stand. "That's it," Pop said after the table incident. "Time to head for the shed."

He said it calmly enough, though, and considering we'd come through the crisis du jour okay, I figured it was looking good to get through this trip with no major disasters.

Famous last words, as Mama would say.

Big Brutus

CHAPTER 6

Welcome challenges! They will exercise your ingenuity.

—Kent Clark, etc.

Next morning, Gee wet the bed again—a delayed reaction to Big Brutus, maybe. Sucking in my first reaction, I scrunched up the sheet and took it along with me to the camp shower, where I threw it on the drain and stomped on it. That helped, and also got the sheet pretty clean, too. When I emerged from the shower, a couple of older girls were standing in front of the mirror doing things to their hair that wouldn't last two seconds in the Kansas wind. One of them asked, "Is that your special blankie?"

All these new challenges were giving my ingenuity a workout: now I had to figure out how to dry a very wet sheet. Since Pop was ready to hit the road, the best solution seemed to be to tie it—really tight—to the hatch handle at the back of the RV, and let 'er flap. At our first pit stop, I'd scoot back there and take it down before he noticed.

But when we stopped at a town called Medicine Lodge, the sheet was gone. Wind power really is something.

I could always buy another sheet, but your average convenience store wasn't likely to stock them alongside the Cheez-Its. And convenience stores were about all this town had to offer, aside from the home of Carry Nation, who used to smash up saloons and liquor bottles with a

This is Big Brutus. He is hugealistic. He is giantanimous. There's a big shovel part that looks like a mouth. Gaaaooowp! There's all these holes inside you can disappear from. I climbed up it on the outside and felt all floaty like a balloon. Then I went POP!

Love, Gee Sparks

Mama—He didn't really pop, and neither did Pop. Ha! We're all fine. Having a great time wish you were here, etc. X, Ronnie hatchet. Gee wanted to meet her, until he found out she was dead.

"That's the problem with a lot of the people we'd like to meet," Pop remarked as he turned onto the highway heading north. We were getting to the part of the map that showed lots of white space between towns. And the towns were mostly small print, meaning something like Partly, MO: hardly a shopping mecca. Pratt was the nearest bold-print town. Farther west lay Greensburg, with the tiny red letters indicating a special attraction: WORLD'S LARGEST HAND-DUG WELL. That sounded like the kind of thing Pop might stop for . . . but risky. Imagine explaining to Mama how Gee fell down the world's largest hand-dug well.

I glanced up just as a billboard for HISTORIC FRONT STREET flickered by. It was the third or fourth Front Street billboard I'd seen, all showing two guys in Western outfits shooting at each other. Something clicked—I checked the map again, looking for Dodge City. It was definitely bold print, more or less on our way, with tiny red letters to boot: HISTORIC FRONT STREET. That settled it for me. If Dodge City had a Wal-Mart, I wanted to go.

"So what's the big deal about Dodge City?" I asked after a few minutes.

"The big deal about Dodge?" Pop repeated. "Didn't you ever watch *Gunsmoke* on TV?"

"No." I munched a cracker, glancing back at Gee. Big Brutus *had* settled him down, so far. Almost three hours on the road, and he'd just now worked up to playing Carry

Nation, smashing Cheez-Its on the dinette table with baby carrots. "But I've heard of it."

For somebody who didn't watch TV, Pop sure knew his Westerns. For the next thirty miles, he gave me a crash course on the shows that shaped his character while he was growing up: not just *Gunsmoke* (which wasn't even his favorite), but *Bonanza,* and *Have Gun, Will Travel,* and *Maverick*—the whole subject got him pumped. "Maybe we'll stop at Front Street," he added. "It's not far out of the way. Of course it's a tourist trap, but the last time I went through, they had a pretty decent gift shop."

"Dodge City is a real town, right? Not just a tourist trap?"

"Sure. A real cow town. Ranchers used to herd their cattle up from Texas and load 'em on railcars in Dodge or Wichita or Abilene. The cowboys could get pretty wild after weeks on the trail, so all those towns needed a tough sheriff to keep order. Like Wyatt Earp—he was the sheriff of Dodge at one time." (In my opinion, somebody would have to be tough to live up to a name like that.) "There was a TV show about him, too. . . ."

As usual, Pop was hitting his stride just about when my interest started to slip. He went from lawman to outlaw so many times I couldn't tell one from another, but any cow-and-tourist-town had to have some stores, too. I leaned back and squinted my eyes against the glare, thinking up an excuse to stop at one.

This part of Kansas was what people mean when they say *flat.* Even the creeks and ponds were flat, in a way I'd never seen back home. Instead of flowing in ditches or settling into dips, they just kind of lie there, right on the surface, like glass. We rolled past pale-yellow wheat fields so thick the tractor tracks looked like the squiggles you make with your finger on fur. Two cattle trucks passed us, each with a whiff of rolling feedlot: *whoosh, whoosh.*

"Yeah," Pop said. "It might be fun to see ol' Front Street again. We could get there by two, spend a couple hours, and then look for a campsite. You see any on the map, Ronnie?"

I folded the map to a square with Dodge City in the middle, and was looking for the little triangle camp symbols, when Gee suddenly let out a yelp, unbuckled his seat belt, and threw himself at the windshield. "LOOK!"

Pop slammed on the brakes; we slewed to the right and stopped. "Look at that!" Gee yelled, pointing at the long white trailer that had just passed us. It was already too far away to make out the logo on it.

Pop, both hands on the wheel, was breathing deeply but seemed to be in control. Which was more than you could say for me. I grabbed my little brother by the neck and marched him back toward the dinette table. "If you do that again, I'll . . . lock you in the bathroom. All you have to do when you see something is stay put and—"

"But, Ronnie, didn't you see what was on the side of that trailer? It was the Human Cannonball!"

"I don't care if it was the president! What I'm saying is, stop with the yells and the jumping around while we're on the road. Save it for when we stop. You get my point?"

My real point was, if he cut short my RV odyssey, I would have a tough time turning a negative into a positive.

I tried to get this across by staring at him really hard as Pop restarted the RV. Instead of pulling back onto the highway, though, the vehicle rolled slowly forward and stopped again. After a minute, Pop said, "There's something you don't see every day."

I crept forward and stared, trying to figure out what the heck we were looking at. At first glance, it was a long, skinny junkyard stretching for maybe a quarter-mile along the right side of the highway. But the junk was moving. In fact, the junk was shaped and bent and punched and welded into a chorus line of moving parts.

"Whirligigs," Pop said. "Somebody's got a lot of time on his hands."

Each figure was welded to a steel fence post and mounted about three feet from the ground. There were so many it was hard to concentrate on just one at a time, and they didn't seem to have any overall purpose or plan: chickens, tomatoes, rabbits, cornstalks, all kinds of human-like shapes, with only their busy-ness in common. The wind played them like an orchestra. I rolled the window down to listen: *Clank-clank. Whirrrrrr. Buzzzzz.*

"Cool!" Gee yelled, and jumped out the back door. I reached for my own door latch, ready to head him off. Pop caught my eye and shook his head.

Gee was running up to individual creations, where he'd pause for a second, half-crouched, then imitate whatever it was doing. His arms pumped, his feet stamped, his whole body twirled around.

There were a few he couldn't imitate even if he wanted to because—well, let me just say they were both politically incorrect and anatomically incorrect. The guy who made them didn't seem to like anybody in government. Or out of it.

Pop slowly opened his door and slid out, taking his camera. I followed, and watched him get close to one of the whirligigs to take a picture. Then he lowered his camera and just looked at Gee. Here was a cutout of a skinny guy in running shorts, legs turning like a pinwheel, and there was Gee, pinwheeling. Here was a crazy chicken with its head bobbing up and down—and there was Gee, bobbing. Pop turned to me. "He *can't* stop, can he? Any more than they can."

I was afraid this would happen. "He's getting better, really. He just got through second grade with no teacher crack-ups."

That didn't come out right. I meant that no teachers had insisted Gee be transferred to other classes because they couldn't take it anymore. But Pop just said, "They never understand." Then he raised his voice to call out, "Gee! Five minutes, and we're back on the road."

Dodge City is still a cow town, by the smell of it. We had to crawl right through the middle to reach Historic Front Street, competing with cattle trucks and pickups. Pop was getting grouchy about stoplights and drivers who pulled out in front of him and then drove too slow. Gee was getting antsy and I was about to go back and sit on him when we finally pulled into a parking space. Just ahead of us was a high wooden fence, and between the slats of the fence I could see a row of buildings that looked like "the town" in every Western movie ever made: General Outfitters. Livery Stable. Long Branch Saloon. "Is this for real?" I asked.

"The street is real," Pop told me. "But the buildings come right out of *Gunsmoke*."

Gee hit the sidewalk and went straight to the fence. Pop pulled him down. "No more climbing. Remember yesterday?" At the admission gate, he got grouchy again. "Eight bucks apiece?!" he exclaimed. "Just to walk around a fake TV set?"

My grandfather is maybe on the cheap side of thrifty.

"I'm free," Gee said, pointing to the sign.

"No you're not," I corrected him. "It says children under seven, not children seven and under. But there's a family rate, Pop—we're family."

"Twenty-five," he grumbled. "That won't save us anything."

"Well, as long as we're here we could check out the gift shop. You said it was worth seeing." Though I wasn't likely to find bedsheets, unless they had lassos and spurs on them.

It's not true that if you've seen one gift shop you've seen them all. I can personally testify that if you're into Western, Front Street is the place for you: hats, boots, sheriff's badges, guns and holsters, cattle skulls, and kid versions of all that. Plus cowhide rugs, rawhide whips, ranch and farm sets, furniture and picture frames made out of cattle horns, leather everything. Plus posters, books, videos, and DVDs of every Western your grandfather grew up with, and tapes and CDs of every song they played on

those shows. There was even a song about Wyatt Earp—
seriously.

We were in luck at first, because Gee found another
kid his age to play gunfight with, while I perused the postcards. There was one of the whirligigs—"wind sculptures,"
according to the caption—and one of the gunfighters on
Front Street. I snapped those up right away, but then
something different caught my eye. It was a little girl
standing before a field of sunflowers. If she were standing
in the field, she would have been invisible, because their fat
yellow faces towered over her. Monster flowers! They
reminded me of the giant jackrabbit, except for being real.

Gee's friend went out the side door with his family to
visit Front Street, leaving Gee to me until Pop was ready to
go and I could ask to stop at Wal-Mart. "How about a hat?
Here's one that'll fit you." I took a black hat with a snake-
skin band from the display and plopped it on his head: too
big, but that just made him look cute.

He pouted under the wide brim. "I want a golden helmet. Like Cannonball Paul."

"For you, that might be more useful," I agreed.

"Why can't we go out on Front Street?"

"You know why. We don't have tickets. How about a
vest? Look—real leather, with fringe and silver studs. I'll
bet all the cool kids at school will be wearing these next
fall."

No use—he wasn't interested in clothes, unless they
made him look like a gorilla or a superhero. For a while he
amused himself by pressing his nose and lips against the

glass door and blowing his cheeks out until one of the store clerks said, "Little boy, please stop that."

Meanwhile, some of those hats were starting to grow on me. I'm kind of an ordinary-looking person, with straight yellowish-brownish hair and blue eyes and "her father's nose," as Mama says—which meant I could do with a little less nose. But a soft beige hat with a band of silver-and-turquoise medallions kind of puts a nose in perspective.

Kent Clark says to choose clothes that build your confidence. Much as I wanted a car, it would almost be worth buying a horse to go with a hat like that. Besides, you didn't need a license for a horse, right?

Suddenly, it occurred to me that I hadn't heard any of the store clerks say "Little boy please stop that" lately. I listened for falling merchandise or thumps on the floor, but what I heard, over the background of some guy singing "O bury me not on the lone pray-ree," was Pop in conversation about the power source of the future.

He was in the book section, discussing his new business with a man holding a book about windmills—the old-fashioned kind of windmill that used to pump water on the lone prairie. The fellow Pop was talking to seemed interested—at least he wasn't making excuses to get away. When I ran over, both men looked up. "Where's Gee?" I asked.

My mother and I have this radar when we're all together: if either of us senses danger, we lift our heads like grazing deer and say together, "Where's Gee?" It's not a real question—it's a signal. Pop hadn't learned that yet, so he answered, "How should I know?"

I started a quick search of the store, and after giving the other man his business card, Pop joined me. "I don't think he's in here," I said.

"Not out there, either." We paused beside the glass door leading to Historic Front Street. In the dusty road outside the livery stable, a couple of dudes in Old West outfits were shouting at each other as a crowd of spectators gathered. Evidently they were gearing up for a gunfight, just like on the billboards.

"He couldn't get out through this door," Pop said. "It has an automatic lock."

Back to the parking lot, then. I wasn't in full panic mode yet. Gee had the sense by now not to run out into traffic, or any of the usual little-kid tricks. The problem was with *un*usual kid tricks. We searched the parking area and the RV while people lined up on the sidewalk to watch the shoot-out. I was starting to feel just a little edgy when—

Pow! Pow!

The gunfire was so loud it made me jump. But what followed was a shriek, all too familiar: "You got me! I'm a goner!"

I ran to the fence, and sure enough Gee was staggering around, clutching his stomach and throwing in a few moves he'd picked up from the whirligigs. The gunman who was still standing looked clueless for a minute, then put one hand on his hip and shook his head. The dead man rolled over to find out who was stealing his scene. Then he sat up and said something that made the spectators laugh.

Unfortunately, Gee doesn't know when to quit. He flopped on his back in the dust and jerked his legs like a frog, then rolled on his stomach and gouged the dirt with his toes. Finally, the dead guy stood and hauled him up by the shoulder.

"Okay, folks—who's willin' to lay claim to this varmint?"

Pop and I looked at each other. So much time went by I got a little nervous. I jerked my head in Gee's direction, as though to remind Pop: *Hey! You're the adult here!*

Finally, he waved his hat over the fence and called, "That would be me."

Laughter is a great thing, but being laughed *at* is hard to take. Especially for Pop, I found. When the gunman opened the gate to hand over the offender, Pop grabbed Gee by the collar and pulled him to the RV, opened the coach door, and threw him in. Then he stepped up into the cab and started the engine.

When we were on the highway again, I glanced back at Gee. He had buckled himself in and looked like a perfectly behaved seven-year-old who happened to be covered with a thick layer of road dust. And had a thumb stuck in his mouth. I turned back to Pop, who gripped the wheel with both hands like he was driving a tank. "I guess it was time to get out of Dodge, huh?" I remarked, trying to lighten the mood.

When he didn't answer, I knew we were in trouble.

I can expect the unexpected, but I don't have to like it.

—Veronica Sparks,
I Could Write a Book and Someday I Will

It took a while to find a suitable campground not too close to town. Pop drove to it without saying a word, and Gee didn't say anything, either. Since I don't talk unless there's a good chance of getting an answer, it was a very quiet trip. And a very long one.

To tell the truth, I was a little disappointed in my grandfather. Not for getting mad at Gee, which was perfectly understandable. But however difficult Gee was, we were still Pop's flesh and blood, and he shouldn't have been tempted to disown us, the way I was pretty sure he'd been tempted back at Front Street. It made me feel cold.

On the upside, we were still headed west.

The campground we finally stopped at had a total of two dozen sites, most of them empty, gathered around a little playground with squeaky swings and a rusty merry-go-round. After Pop had signed in, paid the fee, and parked at the farthest campsite, I opened the RV door and Gee shot out, headed for the playground. Pop spoke, for the first time since leaving Dodge City: "I think we could all use a little break from each other. So for tonight you two can sleep in the tent. A real camping experience—how about that?"

This was the first I'd heard of a tent. It kind of

confirmed his attitude toward us, but I had to admit a little space sounded good to me, too. And it would temporarily solve my problem—which I suddenly remembered—of the missing bedsheet. We got out of the cab and Pop opened up the storage garage at the back of the Coachman, where all kinds of stuff was stored on shelves or hung on Peg-Board hooks: tools, lawn chairs, spare tire, even a garden hose. He tossed a tent, sleeping bag, and cot on the ground.

I helped spread the tent and thread the poles through the sleeves on top of the dome. My mood was going wobbly, so I tried to affirmatize my attitude.

"This'll be fun!" I set one end of the pole into the foot pocket and held it steady as he raised the tent. "We used to go camping all the time with Daddy. Gee wouldn't remember. We had one of those ridgepole tents with a divider. Mama called one side the living room and the other side the bedroom. On our last trip it rained for two days straight. We sat in the living room and played dominos, and then Daddy put on some music and we all danced. Only Daddy was way too tall to stand up in the tent, so we danced on our knees! I remember him doing all these disco moves, and it was so funny. . . ."

My point was to show Pop we were gung ho for anything he cared to dish out, but talking about Daddy for any length of time always made me suddenly want to stop talking. About anything. In a voice meant to sound chipper, I changed the subject. "So, what do you want for dinner— hot dogs or mac and cheese?"

Pop snapped the rain-fly poles in place and tied the last

corner down. He seemed to be going out of his way not to look at me. "Tell you what. I'll fend for myself tonight and you just fix something for you and Gee."

"Well, can I come in long enough to use the stove, at least?" The question came out a little sarcastic, I'll have to admit.

"Sure. Sure. Whatever you need." He unzipped the tent door and threw the sleeping bag inside. "Sorry I don't have two bags, but the cot's not bad to sleep on. I'll show you how to set it up."

"That's okay. I can figure it out." All of a sudden I needed a break from him as much as he did from us. With my chin up, I marched down to the seedy-looking playground. Gee was playing king-of-the-hill on the merry-go-round with two other boys as wired as he was. It looked to me like somebody was sure to be killed. But I just sat on one of the two swings—the kind with the butt-squeezing rubber seat—and pushed myself back and forth while the chain squeaked and grumbled overhead. There was a pay phone at the end of the drive, and this would have been a good time to call home, except that I couldn't trust my voice just then.

Note to me: there are some things I should never, ever talk about. Especially when my mood is wobbly.

By the time Gee's new friends went home to their campsite, and I dragged him back to ours, the sun was swinging low and we could tell Pop had been busy. The fire he'd started on the grate had burned down to coals, the sleeping bag was rolled out on one side of the tent, and the cot was set up on the other, with pillows and blankets, and a lantern hanging from the center hook. The cooler was stocked with cans of Dr Pepper, bunches of grapes, and a package of hot dogs. Hot dog buns and a bag of marshmallows were stacked on the cooler so we could have our own wiener roast. Pop must have walked to the campground store, because the marshmallows and soda weren't part of our stock.

I would have thought it was really nice of him, except for the fact that he'd kicked us out like cats.

"Oh boy!" Gee yelled. "This'll be fun!"

He wanted to invite his other-side-of-the-campground friends, but that sounded like more fun than I could stand. I talked him into a nice quiet dinner for two, and it stayed mostly quiet until he caught his hair on fire with a flaming marshmallow. Just a little fire—half a can of Dr Pepper put it right out.

The sun set while all this was going on, but Gee didn't notice until it was time to walk to the showers. Once there, I had to send him back in twice before he got all the Front Street washed off. On the walk back to our campsite, he dropped our flashlight and the batteries fell out. I caught one, but the other rolled into a ditch. We went on in the dark, with security lights every fifty feet to show us the road. Clouds rolled spookily across the moon.

Our little tent looked sad and abandoned when we finally reached the campsite. One light glowed in the bunk window of the RV, where Pop must have been reading in bed. That made me think of reading a bedtime story to Gee, as Mama sometimes did to settle him down after a wild day. But Pop hadn't thought to leave us any books, and I sure wasn't going to knock on his door and ask for one.

The wind was picking up, blowing fluffy white cottonwood seeds off the trees. A gusty ghost-shape swirled by.

"I've changed my mind," Gee announced. "I want to sleep inside after all."

No point in reminding him of the cold hard facts. "No, this'll be *fun*." I unzipped the tent door and crawled in. "Come on—you take the cot. It'll be like sleeping on a trampoline."

Not a smart thing to say, because of course he wanted to bounce on the cot. After he flipped it over on himself, he settled down long enough to dictate a postcard to me—the "wind sculpture" one—and stayed mostly on topic. Then we played a few rounds of Go Fish with the cards Pop had thoughtfully packed in our overnight supplies. Poker would have been my choice, but Gee had trouble remembering whether a straight beat a flush or vice versa.

Once he was tucked in bed, I started the good-night song Mama used to sing to him, but he cut me off: "Hey! I'm not a baby."

"Okay. Good night, sleep tight, don't let the bedbugs bite."

" 'Night, Ronnie."

I turned the lantern out and wiggled down into the sleeping bag. After a minute, he said, "Ronnie?"

"Huh?"

"Do you think there's any bedbugs in here?"

"Nope. The door zips up, remember? Nothing can get

in here. Besides, if they do they'll get me first. You're the one that's off the ground."

"Okay." A few minutes crawled by, bedbug-like, while the wind sucked the tent walls in and out, in and out. "I don't want anything to get you, Ronnie."

I sighed. "Won't happen. It was a joke, all right?"

"Oh. Okay."

He was quiet for a while. Everything was so quiet, I could hear our eyelids blinking. After a while, I must have dozed off, but it didn't feel like I'd been asleep any time at all when Gee said, "We're blowing away."

The wind had kicked up. In fact, several winds had kicked up, and they were all playing tag around the tent. Our tent didn't want to play. Its sides drew in and puffed out with every shift in wind direction, and I could feel the forces of nature tugging at the stakes that Pop had pounded in just a few hours ago. They were holding on by their slender aluminum fingernails. "We're not going to blow away," I said.

"How do you know? We're gonna be picked up and spinned around and around and set down in some place we've never seen before."

"You've watched *The Wizard of Oz* too many times. Things like that don't really happen."

"They do too! Ever heard of a tornado? One time I saw a picture of a whole tree picked up and stuck in a house like a toothpick!"

"This isn't a tornado. It's just wind." The wind poofed and the tent shuddered as the rain fly slid all the way back: *scriiiiiitch*. I could see it hovering over the back window like a droopy eyelid, and next minute felt rain splashing in from the front. "Shoot! That's all we need." I got up to zip both windows shut, then crawled back into the sleeping bag. Rain pelted down in big fat drops, first like bullets from a single-shot .22 rifle: *ping! ping! ping!* Then *rat-tat-tat-tat-tat*, like a machine gun.

"What's that noise?" Gee whispered.

"It's raining, dummy!" Usually I don't call him names, since he gets enough of that at school, but my nerves were pretty strained by then. Pop could have at least come out to see if we were okay. The stupid zipper pull on the rear window rattled in the wind, and it sounded like a mocking laugh: *huh-huh-huh.*

"No," Gee said, still whispering. "It's not the rain, it's . . . a creature. It's right outside. And it's . . . snortling. Can you hear?"

I listened closer but wasn't sure if I heard what he was talking about. "It's probably just the rain fly. It slipped over where it's not supposed to be."

"Oh," he said. A minute later, he said, "It's still where it's not supposed to be. Maybe you ought to go fix it."

"Oh, right—in the dark, in the rain. No, thanks. Just go to sleep."

Splatter-patter. Huh-huh-huh. Snort-snortle. Just go to sleep, I told myself.

Then Gee yelped and turned the cot over. Next minute he was burrowed up against me, clutching his blanket and shaking so hard his teeth rattled. "It moved!"

"What moved?"

"That thing that's outside the tent! I felt it, and it's *big*!"

Nothing like a night in the great outdoors!

Gee whimpered, "I want to go inside."

Me too—but that would be caving, saying we couldn't take it and giving Pop an excuse to cart us back to Missouri. "You probably felt the wind pushing in."

"No! There's a creature out there!"

"Listen, do you want to go home and tell Casey you were too scared to spend a whole night in a tent? Or would you rather tell him that you spent all night outside in an almost-tornado? I'll bet he's never done that."

Gee didn't answer, but he snuggled a little closer. I had to admit, he felt a little like a teddy bear on a scary night— though squirmier than most.

I guess we wore ourselves out enough to sleep, because dawn light woke me up. That, and a noise outside the tent.

Slowly I turned toward the east and the pale pink glow throwing silhouettes against the nylon wall. The rain fly still sagged over the zipped-up window. And underneath it was a hulky, bearlike shape.

I bolted upright in the sleeping bag. First thought: there really *was* something out there! And second thought: it ate my brother! But then came the unmistakable sound of Gee whispering, which is louder than most people talking. Easing out of the bag, I crept through the open door of the tent, then stood up and tiptoed around the corner.

What had seemed like only one creature was really two—my brother and a big shaggy dog with a thumpy tail.

Gee looked up at me with a huge grin and said, "His name is Leo. And he's *mine.*"

He'd always wanted a dog but couldn't have one, because since Daddy died, every place we'd lived had a "no pets" policy. His asthma was a factor, too, though less of one now. Mama told him she'd think about it when we moved to Partly, but so far she'd had too many other things to think about. I knew she thought a dog would be good for Gee—teach him responsibility, be a loyal companion, and all that—but I was pretty sure she had something a little smaller in mind.

As for me, I don't have anything against dogs, but never especially wanted one. They're messy and in the way, and more so the bigger they are. This dog looked like he could stop a truck.

"He's probably covered with fleas!" I said. "We're going to have to spray you with Raid before you get back in the RV!"

At the sound of my voice, the dog scootched back and hung his head. "You hurt his feelings!" Gee said.

"Pop's gonna hurt more than that." My eye fell on an empty hot dog package. "You didn't feed him, did you?"

Stupid question. I stepped closer and pushed aside the long hair on the dog's neck, while he wiggled his butt like he was trying to corkscrew himself into the ground. "He has a collar," I said. "That means he belongs to somebody. Maybe somebody in this campground."

"But he doesn't have any tags!"

"How do you know his name, then?"

"I just do. Right, Leo? Whoever he belonged to turned him loose, and now he belongs to me."

The dog burrowed his nose into Gee's chest as if begging, *Protect me!* Like he didn't even know he could have me for lunch. I sighed. "Somehow I don't think Pop'll see it that way."

No surprise there. Our kindly old grandpa got up with the sun, chipper as a bluebird after his peaceful night, and emerged whistling from the RV. "So, how'd you two survive? Looks like we got a little rain. We'd better—what the *heck?*"

The sound of a man's voice sent the dog straight to Panic City. He lunged out of Gee's arms and made a bolt for the trees, where he stood quivering like a cornered mouse. "Where'd that thing come from?" Pop demanded.

Gee explained, sort of: "He's a dog and he stayed by our tent last night and he likes me and I want to keep him! Please?"

Pop was shaking his head even before Gee got to the "I want" part. "No way, José."

"But *why?*" The "why" came out long and whiny.

Pop started ticking reasons off his fingers. "Number one: I couldn't afford to feed him. Two: no place to keep him. Three: he's probably loaded with fleas. Four: he's been spooked. Whoever had him before probably didn't treat him right, and that's why he's so jumpy. Watch this." Pop stamped a foot toward the dog and clapped his hands sharply. "SCRAM!" Leo whirled and ran, then turned back, whining.

Pop's reasonable reasons just made Gee wail louder.

While we packed up the tent, he was clutching Leo under the trees as though he'd never let go.

"Before we take off, he's going to the shower," Pop told me. I knew he meant the boy, not the dog. "And be sure he washes his hair."

So I dragged Gee off to the shower, and then back to the RV, where Pop was impatiently waiting for us. The dog had crept closer, inch by inch, until he crouched on the edge of the campsite, thumping his tail. I took Gee firmly by the arm and pulled him up the steps. Pop lobbed a rock in Leo's direction, yelling again, "Scram!"

Gee dissolved in tears then, and I decided to sit with him until the crisis was over. When we pulled out of the campsite, I caught a last glimpse of the dog, looking so sad and lonesome I could almost forget about the fleas.

These are whirligigs. Pop says like me. They look like they grew from crazy seeds. They go rattle! Snap! There's this guy with legs that go in a circle and the wind blows them around and around and around and around. Run run run run. Like me. Rattle! Snap! Good night.

Love, Gee Sparks

Mama—Just like he said. We're camping out while Pop gets some peace and quiet. It's fun! xx, R

8

Don't be afraid to expand your community.
Even the hottest team needs a dash of new blood
now and then.

—Kent Clark

When Gee gets really, really upset, he either pitches a screaming fit or he shuts down like a Game Boy with a dead battery. Since we were on the road, I was relieved when he didn't throw himself on the floor and rearrange the furniture. But the shutdowns are just as bad in a way, like that instant during a lightning storm when everything goes still and you realize the electricity's off.

He sat across from me at the dinette table, clutching a rolled-up piece of paper. When I asked, he un-clutched it just enough for me to recognize the Human Cannonball promotional card he'd picked up in the Big Brutus gift shop. That's one of his little quirks: when he was younger, and he got anything new, he would take it to bed with him for the first night. I mean *anything*. I've seen him sleeping with bundles of socks or toothbrushes still in the package. In moments of stress, he still grabs his latest special thing and cuddles up for dear life, even if it's something spiky like a G.I. Joe action figure loaded with bayonets.

I hate it when he makes me feel guilty, like maybe I should have spoken up for Leo. "Want to play Go Fish?" I asked. He shook his head. "Battleship?" He shook it even harder. "How about that game Mama taught us, where you look for all the letters of the alphabet in highway signs, but you have to find them in order?"

His answer was to unbuckle his seat belt and drop out of sight below the table. When I looked, he was curled around the table leg, still hugging that goofy card.

I moved up to the passenger seat. Pop took an open bottle from the cupholder and offered it to me. "Vitamin C?" I shook my head. He already told me he took one C tablet per day for general immunity, but since this trip began he seemed to be increasing the dosage. "Is Gee okay?"

"He's asleep." After a pause, I added, "Neither one of us slept much last night."

"Hmmm," was his reply.

If I was fishing for an apology, he wasn't biting. I leaned my head back and watched the road through half-closed eyes.

The land stretched out in all directions like it had nothing to hide. And not much to show, either. Overhead a bunch of clouds moved in the same direction as the wind, but slower. Each cloud cast a clean-cut shadow on the ground, all nearly the same size and about an equal distance apart. They were like a huge flock of sheep that happened to be grazing three hundred feet off the ground. Kansas was full of this kind of stuff, like the flat ponds and the trees that all bent one way—all natural, but just a little . . . weird. I was trying to think how to describe it to Mama.

"Hey," Pop spoke up. "*You* didn't want to keep that dust mop of a dog, did you?"

"Nope." Not for myself, anyway—too big, too hairy, too scaredy-cattish.

"Good." My eyelids drooped as the straight horizon blurred. There was one tree at the right corner of the windshield—just one, and it looked like the only tree in the world. "We're headed for southwest Kansas, but there's a wind farm on the way I want to take a look at. The only one in the state—so, far, that is. . . ."

To tell you the truth, wind power was not a spellbinding subject to me just then. I was asleep even before he got going.

I woke up, only a little later, when we pulled into a gas station in some town. The towns all looked pretty much alike—what made them special was that they were so far apart. After an hour of open empty landscape, you're *hungry* for a Conoco sign or a stoplight. "This is the last pit stop between now and noon," Pop said. "Make the most of it."

He got out and unholstered the nearest gas nozzle. Gee woke up mad, bucking my hand off his shoulder when I tried to steer him out the door. Instead of racing for the convenience store like always, to load up on sugar snacks that I would make him put back, he stalked toward the back of the RV. Then he stopped short with a gasp.

From the motorcycle trailer came a sound I knew well already: a thump and a whine. Cozied up to Pop's Yamaha was a big shaggy dog.

Gee grasped the situation quicker than I did. Grabbing

Leo's collar, he hissed, "Come on, boy! You've gotta hide!" That seemed as do-able as sticking a Lay-Z-Boy recliner under your mattress. Leo was halfway under the rear axle of the Coachman when Pop caught him, alerted by the sound of a tail thumping.

Gee threw his arms around the dog's neck. "See? He wants to keep us, too. Pleeeeease?"

Leo squeezed up against Gee, shivering, like he thought he was no bigger than a chihuahua. It was a sight to melt the stoniest heart, but Pop's heart was granite; all he said was, "If you want anything, get it now." Then he marched off to the store.

Gee crawled from under the RV and squatted on the curb, still hugging Leo. "Pop's not going to change his mind," I told him. "I'm sorry, but after all, he only agreed to two fellow travelers, not three." Gee just clung harder. Shaking my head, I wandered over to the bench next to the store entrance, where a chunky young guy was drinking a Coke.

His shirt had A-1 AUTO embroidered on one pocket and CLINT on the other. He remarked, "Picked up a stray, huh?"

"He picked us up. Or not all of us, just my brother."

"Uh-huh." A minute passed. "Probably full of fleas."

This seemed to be everybody's first thought. "I don't think so. If he was, we'd all be itching our heads off by now."

"Huh." Clint was a man of few words.

After a while, Pop came out with a bottle of Diet Mountain Dew and a doughnut bag. I guess he figured that if his supplements kept him healthy, his food wouldn't have to. When he saw my companion, he paused and pulled a five-dollar bill out of his wallet. "Clint, can you do me a favor? Hold that dog until we're five minutes down the road. Then you can let him go."

"Sure, man." Clint stood up and ambled over to the Coachman, where Pop literally had to pull Gee and Leo apart, handing the boy to me and the dog to Clint. Leo whined and Gee yelled, but old Granite-Heart didn't even seem to hear.

After Pop moved around to the driver's side, I felt a tap on my shoulder. Turning, while Gee struggled in my arms, I came face to face with Abraham Lincoln. On the five-dollar bill, I mean. "Give this back to him at your next stop," Clint said. Then he winked. "Every kid needs a dog."

I wasn't sure *I* needed a dog. But what if Leo's long-term goal of finding a master had been rewarded? After a second, I nodded to Clint and whispered a few words to Gee, who shut off like a faucet.

For the next leg of our trip, Gee looked like he was holding three aces and trying not to show it. Pop was probably too grateful for the silence to notice. I sat up front and worried that all we'd done was prolong the agony. What if at our next stop Pop simply tied Leo to a tree and drove off? The tree wouldn't have sentimental thoughts about boys and dogs, and Gee would have gained nothing but another heartbreaking good-bye. Of course, I thought, scanning the landscape, Pop would have to *find* a tree first. . . .

Or what if we just kept hiding the dog? Not a likely

scenario. Besides, we had to feed him, and there was no money in the budget for a mountain of hot dogs.

Gee kept jumping up to get glasses of water or go to the bathroom until Pop yelled that he'd run the tank dry if he didn't sit down and stay down. When Gee buckled himself in for the fifth or sixth time in less than thirty minutes, I slipped back to the dinette table and said, nice and low, "Okay, tell me: how are you going to hide a furball as big as a Volkswagen?"

"No problemo!" He wiggled with joy. "As soon as we stop, I'll jump out the door and run to the back and pull Leo between the back tires. And you keep Pop busy so he won't notice."

"He won't notice you snuggled under the RV with Bigfoot?"

He sighed, as if I were the one being unreasonable. "I won't *stay* under. I'll just tell Leo to stay until we get moving again. Then he can jump back on the trailer."

"Since when do you speak Dog?"

He just grinned, and I wondered if I was being too negative. Suddenly, my stomach flipped—the RV was slowing down! Then it slowed more, even though a quick glance out the window showed me nothing but flat plains and barbed-wire fence.

"Battle stations!" I hissed. Gee's eyes got big, and he jumped up so fast I had to grab his shirt. "But wait till we come to a full and complete stop."

The full and complete stop happened right after, and he bolted out the door just as Pop turned around to say, "Behold the future!"

I moved up to the passenger seat, and my jaw dropped.

There must have been hundreds of them, stretched into the sky, set in perfectly straight and even rows like sunflowers planted by a finicky gardener. They were such a pale gray that the rows farthest away sort of dissolved into the white horizon. Each one had three blades near the top, some turning fast, some slow, some not at all. Even though I knew they were windmills, all those tall, silent poles in rows looked like they might have been planted by space invaders. Did they come in peace, or what?

"Let's get out and take a look," Pop suggested.

That brought me back to the immediate problem. When he opened his door, I scooted out the passenger side and peeked under the back wheels. Gee was there, holding Leo's tail to keep it from thumping. I gestured frantically for him to come out and leave the dog, while he shook his head, equally frantic, waving me forward to distract Pop.

But Pop didn't need distracting. "Just listen!" he said when I joined him. The blades turned with a steady *row-row-row* and a faint metal buzz.

"How come they're moving at different speeds?" I asked.

"Wind doesn't hit 'em all the same. You can see a few where the blades aren't turning at all—they might be stalled. It's not a very windy day, for here."

You could have fooled me. Little pellets of sand were blasting my legs, and black-eyed Susans along the road nodded like crazy old ladies. "Are they working right now, or just on really windy days?"

"They're working all the time, blowing up enough power for this whole county."

"And you're going to look for another spot like this?"

"Yep. Starting tomorrow, I'll do some reconnaissance. We'll camp at Meade Lake for three, four days while I take readings. Think you kids can stay out of trouble?"

"Uh-huh." With him being gone so many hours in a day, it might be easier to keep Leo out of sight. A cloud of dust approached us on the farm road, and I watched it just because it was the only thing happening on the ground. That is, until I glanced behind me and saw way too much happening: namely, Gee chasing the dog around clumps of prairie grass, trying to get him back under the RV. Leo would let him get close enough to grab his collar before breaking loose again, like it was a big game. At least he had the sense not to bark—Leo, that is.

"Where's Gee?" Pop asked.

"He's okay—just running off some steam," I said quickly. "Look, Pop—somebody's headed our way."

The cloud of dust rolled closer and coughed up a blue-and-white pickup truck. It slowed to a stop as the driver pulled even with us. "Are y'all having car trouble?"

I glanced at him—then glanced again. Under that John Deere cap was a kid not much older than me, sitting kind of low in the cab but leaning his left arm on the window and his right hand on the wheel like he'd been driving all his life.

"No car trouble, son," Pop said heartily. "Just admiring your windmills."

"They're not mine, sir," the boy said with a little smile.

"I don't even like 'em that much. When the wind's real strong, they keep me awake at night."

While Pop reassured him about the wave of the future, I looked way down the road to where a ranch-style house crouched under the towering windmills, like it was terrified of its own crop. Glancing behind me again, I caught sight of a dog's tail and a boy's legs chasing back toward the road.

"Well, good luck," the boy in the truck was saying as he shifted gears. My head snapped around when he said, "Nice dog."

"Yeah, it's a real nice day. Have a good one."

Pop didn't seem to hear that little exchange. The boy squinted at me but didn't say anything as he revved the accelerator and rolled on. Another quick glance showed me that Gee had just about succeeded in herding Leo back to his hideaway, so I distracted Pop a little more. "That kid was just a kid! How come he's driving?"

"Farm-state laws. You can get your license at fourteen or fifteen. Makes sense out here—there's not much to hit." He raised his voice. "Gee! Wherever you are, get on board—we're leaving!"

I didn't see either the boy or the dog, but as soon as Pop walked around to the driver's side, they popped out on the passenger side, with Gee still chasing a happy, loopy Leo. Hearing Pop's door slam, I opened the RV door for Gee. He climbed in all sweaty, giving me a high five while Leo sat in a clump of black-eyed Susans, swishing his tail. I could tell just by looking at him that he knew the drill: as soon as we started rolling, he'd hop on board.

Kent Clark talks about expanding your community, but he probably didn't have mutts in mind. Instead of one hyper traveling companion, I now had two. Our little community had expanded to a little madhouse.

By the time we got to the state park, I had a plan. Sneaking a piece of nylon rope from the storage bin under the sofa, I whispered to Gee, "When we pull up to the campsite, you need to distract Pop somehow. Somehow that doesn't make him mad. I'll tie this rope to the dog's collar and take him—I don't know, somewhere out of sight—and tie him up. Then we'll take it a step at a time, okay?" Gee nodded with his whole body and grinned as wide as Big Brutus.

But first we had to get past the check-in station. The park supervisor was a nice-looking middle-aged lady with curly blond hair, a sparkly smile, and equally sparkly glasses. Guessing that Pop was going to drag out the registration process, I told Gee to stay put, then got out of the cab and stood near the back of the RV, meaning to block any view the lady might have of a dog huddled on the bike trailer. When Pop said something about "my grandkids," I smiled and waved but didn't move away.

Finally, he said, "Well, I guess that's it," and stepped back from the window. I waited until he had crossed in front of the cab and opened the driver's door before leaving my post. Then I realized that when we rolled by the registration hut, that curly-haired lady was sure to see a big wad of fur on the motorcycle trailer. After which, she might chase us down to demand why Pop didn't mention the dog.

But a miracle happened: she took off her glasses to wipe her eyes! I jumped in the cab, hollering, "What a great place! Let's hurry and find our campsite."

"Whoopee!" Gee echoed from the back. "Let's go!"

We almost overdid it; Pop took the time to look me over. "Is ADHD contagious?"

I just smiled, and he put the RV in gear. The lady was now cleaning her glasses. Almost home free! These challenges were starting to be fun.

"Supposed to be some good fishing here," Pop remarked as we followed a winding road around the lake. "Maybe if I have time, I'll teach you and Gee to fish."

"Great!" Fishing had always looked to me like the world's most boring sport, but never mind. While he looked for the ideal camping spot, I was scouting ideal hideouts for a large dog: Wastewater dump? Cluster of cottonwood trees? One rather large bush? We rolled past a fifth-wheel trailer covered with pop-outs, past an extended family of Asians with three vehicles and five tents and kids running all over the place, past a retired couple reading magazines under a screened canopy surrounded by potted geraniums—finally pausing by the farthest slot on the loop.

"A long walk to the shower," Pop said. "But at least we'll have some peace and quiet."

Some of us might, I thought. My busy eyes were casing the place even before the RV stopped, coming to rest on a sign that said HIKING TRAIL. "It's perfect!" I exclaimed. The brushy territory beyond the sign ought to have something stout enough to tie Leo to.

I winked at Gee, said, "I have to go," and popped out of the passenger door. While the Coachman paused, then started slowly backing up, I squeezed onto the bike trailer beside Leo. He cringed but stayed put while I slipped the nylon rope through his collar and tied it in a square knot, muttering, "Come on, boy. Think of it as an adventure."

When the RV stopped, Gee raised a yell that sounded like he'd been attacked by a giant crawdad: "HELP! I'm STUCK!" Pop yelled back, and I made a note to remind Gee that distractions didn't have to be LOUD.

"Come on, boy!" I leapt off with the rope in hand, but Leo didn't. His butt hugged the trailer so tight I nearly fell on mine. And he wouldn't budge. "What's wrong with you, you idiot dog!" Another note: make friends with idiot dog or you'll never be able to do anything with him. I looped the end of the rope around the awning strut and popped back inside the RV, where Pop was ordering Gee to pipe down and be reasonable.

I scurried over to unbuckle Gee's seat belt, whispering, "He's still on the trailer. Take him down the hiking trail and tie him to a bush—quick!" Gee stopped his distraction long enough to give me an enormous wink, then scooted out the back door. I made a lunge to close it before Leo's happy whines could come through, meanwhile babbling, "This is a great park, Pop! Did you see the beach? I can't wait to—"

"All right, you can stop yelling. What's got into you kids?"

"And the grass!" I pointed out the left side of the RV while a dog and a boy raced madly off to the right. "Isn't that great grass? This is real Kansas prairie! What do you want for dinner?"

He just rolled his eyes and said a heaping hot plate of sanity would be nice.

CHAPTER
9

Always be ready to accept a certain amount of risk.

—Kent Clark
(easy for him to say)

We pulled it off. That is, Pop didn't work up enough curiosity to wonder why Gee loaded his plate with chicken—twice—or why he kept running off into the brush or why he wanted to sleep in the tent again. ADHD kids were unpredictable, right? That's why Pop was okay with setting up the tent for him, so Gee could be unpredictable outside. I knew who'd be sharing that tent, and it wasn't me.

Pop turned in early: "Vacation's over. Back to work tomorrow."

In the morning he gave me a list of things not to do, then roared off on his Yamaha, with the equipment for setting up three temporary weather stations bundled on the back fender. "The first item on my agenda," I told Gee, "is to give this dog a bath."

"Okay," he said, happy as a clam. "How?"

We put on our swimsuits and hit the shower, where Gee hung on to Leo's collar while I dumped half a bottle of shampoo on him. Throughout, the dog made a noise like a rusty hinge—a really *loud* rusty hinge. I'd never heard him bark, which made me wonder if all the bark had been kicked out of him. But even the whine was getting on my nerves by the time I'd hit the shower knob about three dozen times.

After that, we tried calling Mama from the pay phone but couldn't get a ring. "Did she forget to pay the phone bill again?" I wondered. Leo shook himself and gave me another shower, so we took a nice long walk in the sunshine while the breeze dried our swimsuits and Leo strained on his nylon leash. We walked all the way to the swimming beach and circled the "primitive" campground (where Gee looked for primitive campers in loincloths and fur but didn't see any). We were on our way back when a lady buzzed toward us on a little Italian scooter. It was the park superintendent, her glasses flashing in the sunlight.

"Hey there," she said, coasting to a stop. "Where's that good-looking grandfather of yours?"

Pop as a hottie?! It took me a minute to choke out, "He's working."

That led to an explanation of what he worked at, which I could handle pretty well by now. She seemed doubtful about our good-looking grandfather leaving us alone in a strange campground all day. "That's no big deal," I assured her. "I've been looking after my brother since he was three."

She glanced at Gee, who was trying to teach Leo—by example—to catch butterflies with his teeth. I realized too late that I hadn't given myself such a great recommendation, but the lady didn't pursue it. "By the way, dogs are supposed to be on a leash at all times. But that dog looks like he needs to run once in a while. You can let him loose on the trail now and then, as long as you're close by."

After she motored away, Gee turned a couple of wobbly cartwheels while Leo looked on, interested but puzzled. "She likes us!"

"Uh-huh, but I think she really likes Pop. And if she likes him, she'll want to talk to him, and while they're talking she might mention Leo."

Gee crashed down, flat-footed. "We've gotta stop them talking!"

"Yeah, right. Let's go eat lunch."

Back at our campsite, I made bologna-and-cheese sandwiches, one each for me and Gee and two for Leo, who wolfed them down and then looked at me as if I could pull sandwiches out of my navel. "Our biggest problem is how to feed this mutt."

Gee let him scarf up the last third of his sandwich. "We could just buy a bag of dog food."

"With what? And where? Don't you think Pop might notice if we walk out of the grocery store with twenty-five pounds of puppy chow?"

He giggled. "We'd just say it's kid chow." I was thinking he wasn't going to be much help, when he spoke up again. "We could learn to fish. Pop said he'd teach us."

Not a bad idea. I had to smile: Leo caused some problems but at least they were interesting problems. And he might earn his keep by giving Gee something to do. I couldn't tell yet if the boy wore out the dog, or vice versa.

Pop returned a little before three that afternoon with a bag of groceries but was in no hurry to rush to the water with a fishing pole. "Isn't Sunday supposed to be a day of rest? Let me take a nap first."

So he napped for an hour, then read for an hour, and then he wanted me to help him set up his laptop for recording data. Old people—well, people his age—always complain about computers, like they spoke a different language. If that's true, the recording program was baby talk—really basic. Pop bragged on me for setting it up, though. He even tossed a Frisbee around with Gee while I started supper—for about fifteen minutes, until Gee's returns got too wild and Pop refused to chase them.

Meanwhile, I pinched some raw hamburger for Leo, and cooked up the rest of the package. Gee ate less than half of his. By the time dinner and cleanup was over, it was almost dark and Pop wanted to run the numbers—as he put it—before heading for the shed (as he put it again). "Running the numbers" meant me entering that day's readings into the program as he read them out, then clicking a button to save them. We'd run averages later, when he collected more numbers. Nothing to it, and everybody was happy with the day's work.

But I still had to figure out the care and feeding of an invisible dog.

Next morning, Gee and I went down to the pay phone again and found an OUT OF ORDER sign on it. "At least the problem's not at the other end," I said. "Maybe the park lady would let us— Gee! Get out of the garbage!"

This, as it turned out, was my brother's idea of a snack for Leo, and after some careful rummaging around we laid out a nice little doggie smorgasbord. But I didn't want to make garbage his regular diet. "Somebody could get sick," I said. "There's probably all kinds of germs making baby germs in that potato salad."

After washing our hands in the restroom, we walked

down to the lake, where Gee ran up and down the boat

down to the lake, where Gee ran up and down the boat ramp as though he were launching himself. When he actually did, I made him stop. Then we walked along the muddy bank looking for shells.

"Hey, look!" Gee had found a piece of nylon fishing line stamped down in the mud. When he pulled all the way to the end, a hook popped out so suddenly it almost bit Leo, who whimpered and slunk away.

The hook was a little bent, but plenty sharp. "Maybe we could tie it to a pole," Gee suggested—his third idea in two days.

Deciding it was worth a try, I hunted around for another piece of line to tie to the one we already had. When the line was long enough to throw out, I wondered, "What can we use for bait?"

"Bait?"

"Fish don't go for hooks because they're so nice and shiny. There has to be something juicy *on* the hook, like a worm or a grasshopper."

The worms all seemed to be on vacation, and the few grasshoppers we found didn't want to be caught, so we settled for a piece of hamburger Gee found in the garbage. Then we walked down the nearest pier and threw out our line as far as it would go.

After a while, I said, "Maybe we have to keep throwing." I pulled the line in, only to find the bait gone. Gee thought something ate it, but my guess was it just fell off. "We could try bologna. Or just wait until Pop comes back and ask him to—"

"Hey, look!" Gee yelled. "It's the windy-farm truck!"

He was pointing back toward the boat ramp, where a dusty blue-and-white pickup was backing down. An aluminum johnboat stuck out over the tailgate. I recognized the driver's John Deere cap first, then the boy under it.

He noticed us while sliding out his boat. "Hey."

"What are you doing here?" I blurted.

He was nice enough not to say that he had as much right to be here as we did. "My aunt Melba's the supervisor. I come here to fish. Once or twice a week?"

Gee and I glanced at each other, then back at him. "You do?" I gave what I hoped was a fluttery sigh. "I always wanted to learn how to fish."

His name was Howard Sayles, and his aunt's name was Melba McClintock, and we all agreed she was real nice. He'd be glad to take us out for an hour or so on his boat but didn't think there would be room for the dog. Gee volunteered to stay on shore, which was okay with me. Even though Kent Clark says you should be ready to accept a certain degree of risk, sharing a boat with a hyperactive kid and a paranoid dog is just asking for trouble. Howard loaded up his gear, then helped me aboard, handed me his second-best pole, and pushed away from the ramp. As he hopped in and turned the switch on the trolling motor, I warned Gee, "Be careful—and keep a sharp lookout."

"Keep a lookout for what?" Howard asked as we buzzed out to deeper water.

I decided to level with him. "For our grandfather, in case he comes back early. We're not exactly supposed to have that dog. Pop ran him off a couple of days ago, but

Leo came along anyway." Howard nodded, like he suspected as much. "Is that your truck?"

"Almost. I'm buying it from my dad. Since he got a new one last summer."

"What does your dad do?"

"Oh, we farm," he said, like it should have been obvious. *We* farm—I guess he earned that driver's license. As we swapped our life stories, I started to like the way he talked, even with all the pauses and question marks stuck in. His voice was calm and steady, not tense like my mother's or blustery like Pop's or chattery like Gee's. He was in eighth grade—just a grade ahead of me!

"How do you like it out here?" I asked.

"It's home. How do *you* like it?"

"Well . . . it's different." Our trip so far hadn't made me a big Kansas fan, but I was reserving judgment until the end.

He grabbed a plastic crayon bucket and set it between his knees. When he pulled the lid off, my stomach lurched a little at the squirmy lump of worms inside. "So. Can you bait your own hook? Or not?"

Accept challenges, I told myself. "Sure! I mean, show me?"

He pulled a worm out of the heap and stuck the hook in, kind of parallel to one end. Head end or tail end, what was the difference? Then I tried it, and after the little quiver my worm made when the hook went in, it wasn't bad.

"They don't feel it," Howard said. "Not pain, anyway. This is the most fun they'll ever have." He showed me how to make a cast, by pushing the button thingy on his reel and flicking the rod with his wrist. The line flew out over the water.

"Looks like fun, all right." I imagined his worm yelling "Yippee!" as it soared through the air and splashed into the lake.

It took a few tries for me to get all the steps together: push in, cast, let out, reel in. Meanwhile, Larry (that's what I named my worm) must have been having the time of his life. Trying to look cool and assured, I finally made a perfect cast, except that the line jerked behind me so hard it nearly pulled the rod out of my hand.

"What happened?" I gasped.

"You hooked my boat." When I turned around, Howard was pulling the hook free from the aluminum rim and Larry had disappeared. I felt like taking a dive myself, but he just stuck on another worm and handed it back. "Good thing you didn't hook me."

After a few minutes, I was casting out and reeling in like a pro, almost. The little motor on the boat kept us turning in wide, slow circles while Howard cast from one side and me from the other. After a while, he said, "Trade?" and we switched sides. He caught three perch and promised me the innards for Leo, but my line didn't get any action at all. It wasn't as boring as I'd thought, though. A late-afternoon breeze fanned ripples on the water, and every sound turned liquid. Once we'd slowed down to barely moving, it was like time itself thickened up and made the light and land and water as rich as cake batter.

We stayed within sight of the bank so I could keep an eye on Gee. By now he had stopped throwing sticks for

Leo and was trying to ride him instead. "Is he always like that?" Howard asked.

"Well, let me tell you . . ."

Once I got started, it was hard to stop telling: how Gee screamed for the first six months of his life and wouldn't stay still for the rest of it. How giving him a bottle was like trying to pin down an octopus using only one hand.

"When he started walking, the only way Mama could get anything done outside was to put him in a harness with a long leash and tie it to the clothesline. If she was inside, she tied the leash to an eye hook screwed into the living room floor. One time a social worker from the Division of Family Services came over because somebody reported that we kept Gee tied up. Of course, she didn't have the story straight—there was a lot of area he could reach, including the DFS lady's purse. After he opened it and dropped her car keys down the furnace grate and ate all her Digest-Tabs, she decided to leave us alone.

"When he was three, he figured out how to unbuckle the harness. When he was four, he climbed every chain-link fence in sight. Plus the water tower, the kiddie roller coaster at Six Flags, and . . . oh yeah, the rock wall at First National Bank. At five, he started kindergarten—three times with four different teachers. At six, he tripped the fire alarm at school, the smoke alarm at church, and the sprinkler system at my great-grandmother's nursing home."

Howard gave a low whistle, duly impressed.

"Everybody says there's not a streak of meanness in him," I went on. "He's just all streak, kind of like a Roman candle with no—" Suddenly, the rod jerked in my hand. "What was that?"

"Well," Howard said slowly, "maybe it's a fish."

"What'll I do?"

He reached over and gave my line a quick, firm tug. "That'll set the hook. When you feel the line go slack, reel 'er in."

That wasn't so easy; whatever was at the other end of the line sure didn't want to be caught. We seesawed back and forth until finally it broke the water, a flash of pure fight. "It's a largemouth bass!" Howard shouted. "Maybe four pounds!"

To me it looked *huge.* "You take it!" I thrust the pole at him.

Four pounds may not sound like a lot, but the fish was almost as long as my arm, and all muscle. It flopped so hard it might have flopped right out of the boat if Howard hadn't got a grip on it and worked the hook out. "He's a beauty. Got a name for him, too?"

I grinned. "Dinner."

When I noticed Gee starting to teach Leo how to chase cars, we headed back to the bank with a string of perch and my world-class bass trailing behind. It was turning out to be a perfect day—even for Leo, who got a snack of fish guts and livers when Howard showed me how to clean and scale my catch.

Howard told me how to cook it, too: "First you wrap him up in tinfoil with some butter and sliced onion. After you build your fire and let it burn down to coals? Throw on the fish and listen close. When he stops popping on one side? Turn him over and wait for the other side to get done. Squeeze on a little lemon juice. Nothing better."

That's just what I did. By the time we heard Pop's Yamaha approaching, Dinner was wrapped and ready to go and the fire had burned down to a steady glow. Gee raced out of the brush where he'd been hiding Leo: "Guess what, Pop! Ronnie caught a big ol' bigmouth!"

Pop, who was expecting macaroni and cheese, absolutely beamed when he caught sight of the grill. While we were telling him about Howard and his boat, Melba McClintock motored up on her little scooter. I had to wonder if she'd been watching for the Yamaha.

"Say, Mr. Hazeltine! I hear your granddaughter is quite the fisherman."

Next, the retired gentleman from the fifth-wheel camper next door sauntered over, leading to the kind of buddy-buddy, just-call-me-Jack conversation Pop is good at. After carefully turning my bass on the grill, I joined them. It felt nice and neighborly to stand around just before dinner at twilight, with other campers pausing in their evening walks and Gee making like a frog after the grasshoppers.

That is, until Mrs. McClintock said, "I hate to tell you this, Ronnie, but Dinner is served."

I turned, to a sight I will never forget: one big hairy mutt with his paws in a nest of shredded aluminum foil and the remains of my four-pound prize catch hanging out of his mouth.

Some things are meant to be.

—Veronica Sparks,
whose mother always says that

At first, I was just plain mad: I didn't catch Dinner to be scarfed down by a mutt who couldn't even appreciate fine dining. But that was the least of our problems.

Because Pop was even madder—more than I'd ever seen him. "Didn't I say *no dogs?* What do you think that meant? One dog that I don't see? You kids have just about pushed your limit—"

Leo bolted for his old hiding place under the rear axle and flattened himself like a rug. Gee followed, but before diving under the RV he turned around and screamed, "If you run over him, you'll have to run over me, too!"

If I were Mrs. Mac, I would have gunned my Italian scooter and buzzed away right then, but she was better stuff than that. "Jack, what is it you have against this dog?"

"How about stealing my dinner, for starters? Besides, dogs are nothing but trouble, and they have fleas and they bark."

"Well," she said reasonably, "it wasn't just your dinner. It was Ronnie's, too, and she—"

I spoke up. "This dog doesn't bark or have fleas. And if we hadn't been forced to hide him, he wouldn't have got into the fish. Gee was in such a hurry when we heard you coming, he must've got careless with the rope."

Pop pointed a finger at me. "You mean to say it's *my* fault the dog got loose?"

"Of course not," said Mrs. Mac, putting a hand on my shoulder. "Nobody's blaming you, Jack—"

"They'd better not. They flat-out disobeyed me—I made myself very clear about not taking him, and they brought him along anyway."

"That's *not* what happened." My natural anger mode is sarcastic and huffy, but I tried to chill on the huffy while explaining how Leo had stowed away on the bike trailer, with Clint the A-1 Auto guy as accomplice. "Here's your money, by the way." I pulled the five-dollar bill out of my pocket, but Pop just looked at it like it was a poopy diaper. My story hadn't softened him a bit, but it did earn sympathy with our audience, which had grown while I was telling it.

"Come on, Jack," said Mrs. McClintock. "Have a heart."

Our next-door neighbor chimed in. "Besides, every kid needs a dog. Didn't you ever have a dog, Jack?"

Pop doesn't like to be pushed—and he especially doesn't like to be boxed in, like he was now, with a feisty female on one side and a nosy neighbor on the other. Any attempt to *make* him change his mind only set it harder. I let the huffiness loose, turned away with a sharp sigh, and stomped back toward the campfire to clean up Leo's mess. But a noise from under the RV stopped me: Gee's sobbing. I could barely see him, wrapped around all that fur. It reminded me of how he used to go to bed with a new pair of socks.

But Leo was a lot more than his latest special thing. That dog, I realized, was the only living creature on this earth who could take Gee exactly as he was, without getting frustrated or sending him to the principal's office or lecturing him about thinking before acting.

I turned back to Pop. "How about we play cards for the dog?"

That startled him out of his stubborn expression. "How's that?"

I took a deep breath, making up the deal as it came to me. "Suppose we play a hand of . . . five-card draw. No, three hands. Best two out of three. If I win, we keep the dog. If you win, we try to find him a good home with somebody else."

"That's the spirit!" our neighbor exclaimed. "I like it. Whaddya say, Jack?"

Mrs. Mac spoke almost too soft to hear. "Give it a chance, Jack."

He tightened up his lips, but his eyes shifted to Gee, then back to me. After a few seconds, he untightened enough to say, "Okay."

The audience cheered. Seriously.

We couldn't just sit down and play. Our neighbor, Mr. Bewick, insisted on being the dealer so everything would be fair and aboveboard. Then he went to fetch his camp table for us to play on and brought back not only the table, but also a string of Japanese lanterns, Mrs. Bewick, and the nice couple from the motor home next door. Of course Melba (as she insisted we call her) had to stay, and a family taking a walk around the lake wandered over when the kids recognized us.

An audience wasn't what I had in mind, but maybe, if I lost, one of those people could help us find a home for Leo. While the table was getting set up, I made sure Gee tied the dog firmly to a tree far away from the action.

"I know you're going to win, Ronnie." He hugged me for luck, but then said he couldn't bear watching, and I could just let him know when it was all over.

By then night was falling, and the Japanese lanterns shed a party glow over the site as Pop and I sat down at the table. Mr. Bewick counted out a dozen toothpicks for each of us, then asked me, "You remember what beats what? Want me to write it down?"

I just shook my head. "Pair, two pair, three of a kind, straight, flush, full house."

Mr. Bewick whistled as he snapped the cards. "She's a sharp one, Jack. Watch out."

I didn't feel sharp—I felt sick. Note to me: don't ever propose a game with your little brother's heart on the line. Still, the scene would have been pretty cool if I hadn't been right in the middle of it. Black sky stretched out over our piece of earth, a fog of lightning bugs hovered over the grass, the little crowd murmured happily in the lantern glow. The cards fluttered as Mr. Bewick worked the stiffness out, his hands turning them to a golden blur. Then he spread them in a fan so we could draw to open.

Pop won the draw. After picking up the five cards Mr. Bewick dealt, he tossed out two toothpicks. Of course I had to do the same to stay in, even though I didn't have anything worth betting on. We both drew three cards, then he bet four toothpicks and I folded. He showed his hand: three fives.

"That was too quick," Mr. Bewick said as he shuffled our cards back into the deck. "Let's stretch the next one out a little, okay?"

He gave me a pair of threes this time—something to work with, though not much. Because it was my turn to open, I tossed in one toothpick and drew three cards again. Pop only took one, which made me catch my breath. But when Mr. Bewick dealt me a pair of sevens, I decided to go for it, betting two. Pop threw down his cards, showing he didn't make that straight or flush he was going for.

"Last deal, make it real." Mr. Bewick slapped down my five cards. I was seeing how much I didn't understand about this game yet: we were tied on the best hand, but Pop was ahead on toothpicks. I should have bet at least two more on my pair of threes, and then I would have been ahead. Live and learn, except I had only one more chance to pull this off.

I picked up my five cards: a pair of jacks stared me in the face.

Don't show anything, I said to myself, making a little frown to keep my mouth from turning up. Pop opened with two toothpicks, like he usually did. I asked for three cards and got a pair of fours and a ten. Pop asked for two cards— bad sign. Did he have three of a kind and was drawing for a full house? Or a pair and an ace, or was he bluffing me?

Two pair is a rotten hand—good enough to sucker you into making a big bet, but often not good enough to win.

Even if he didn't get the full house he was probably drawing for, he'd beat me with three of anything, even measly twos.

I looked up at Melba, who was standing behind Pop and might have seen his cards, even though he was holding them close. She didn't even glance my way—this was up to me.

"It's up to you, Ronnie," said Mr. Bewick.

I took a quick breath and tossed out five toothpicks. "Ah," murmured the audience as I struggled with my poker face. But Pop matched those, then said, "I'll raise you two."

A bluff, or not? Well, I thought, if I was going to lose, might as well lose big. "I'll see your two," I said, throwing them in, "*and* raise you three." That cleaned me out of toothpicks.

Pop hesitated, then pushed three toothpicks into the pot. "Call. What've you got?"

Slowly, I lay down the pair of fours, then the pair of jacks.

Pop stared at it for a few seconds—seconds that crawled like snails. Then he tossed his cards, facedown. "Beats me."

I let out a breath I'd been holding, as cheers erupted all around me.

A party sort of happened after that, and that's the best kind of party—no hurt feelings over who didn't get invited, no worries over the cupcakes getting burned or the drinks running out or how to keep everybody happy. All that just took care of itself.

Boxes of doughnuts and six-packs of Pepsi and beer showed up, along with crackers and a cheese ball. Neighbors drifted in and drifted out, and for that night only they were all our new best friends. While accepting my umpteenth congratulations for winning the poker game, I realized that this event was because of *me*. I mean, more or less. And the funny thing was, it didn't come about because of any long- or short-term goals or rowing the flow. I'd just had a flash of inspiration, and who knows where those flashes come from?

For most of the party, Gee stayed with Leo, except for when he dashed out to hug me while everybody around us said, "Awwwwww." That's what he was doing—hugging, I mean—when a big white trailer pulled by a white pickup slowly circled the campground. Not many people noticed, because Mr. Bewick's other-side neighbors had brought over a polka CD, and my grandfather and Melba were showing the kids how it's done. Suddenly, Gee screamed as though an alligator had crawled up from the lake and bit him on the leg.

Then he took off after the trailer. Before the guests could wonder if he was in trouble or just insane, I yelled, "I'll get him!"

He made me work at that, but I finally got close enough to grab him by a handful of T-shirt, gasping, "What's got into you?"

"Lemme go!" he yelled, struggling with hyper-kid energy. The trailer up ahead passed under a security light, and I had just enough time to read the gold letters painted across the double doors in back: FASTER THAN A SPEEDING BULLET—

Then it rolled out of sight. "Why'd you stop me?" Gee demanded. He was so frustrated he was stomping with both feet.

"Well, ex*cuse* me, but I haven't seen you chase a vehicle since you were five. What's up with that?"

"What's up with that?" he repeated. "What's up with *that*? Didn't you see? It was CANNONBALL PAUL!"

He wanted to keep running, but when I pointed out that the trailer was already out of sight, he agreed to go back to the campground with me. Very sulky, though, even after I'd won him a dog. That's gratitude.

"Cannonball Paul?" Melba repeated when we asked her about the trailer. "He's been here the last two nights, camping on the other side of the lake. I think he came from some event in Garden City."

Stunned, Gee pulled the card out of his pocket and looked at the back. "But it doesn't say he's *s'posed* to be in Garden City. Does it?"

I scanned the dates. "Nope. Maybe he got that gig after the card was printed up."

"It's not fair! He was here all along and I never knew it!"

He'd forgotten all about Leo. I told him to find a good place to tie up *his* dog for the night. When Gee stomped away, I asked Melba, "Do you know where this cannonball guy is going next?"

"No idea."

I had to admit, it was kind of a bummer to think Mr. Amazing himself had been across the lake from us, and we never even knew it.

This is Dodge City. There are two cowboys. One of the cowboys is Ronnie and the other one is Pop. Ronnie says, This town ain't big enough for the both of us. And Pop says, Draw stranger. POW! Ronnie wins.

Love, Gee Sparks

Mama—I'll explain later. We're all getting along fine. R

CHAPTER 11

Sometimes the best things in life just happen.

—Veronica Sparks

Before taking off on his Yamaha the next day, Pop said he'd be home early but he had plans for the evening and we were supposed to leave him alone. And he'd buy one bag of dog food—just one—but otherwise he'd pretend Leo didn't exist and he expected the same consideration from Leo. "And one more thing. That mutt never comes inside the RV. *Ever.* Got that?"

Around nine a.m., Mr. and Mrs. Bewick pulled out, and their other-side neighbors soon after, leaving that end of the campground to us. I spent the morning trying to make friends with Leo, or at least convince him I wasn't his enemy. He'd let me get close enough to scratch his ears, but then he'd shake his head and back off.

Gee started a stick-chasing class, but the dog never seemed to catch on—even when Gee hurled a stick and chased it himself. "Why don't you teach him to throw instead?" I suggested as Gee trotted up with the stick in his teeth. "You could do the fetching."

"Ha, ha, *ha!*" This was his idea of a sarcastic laugh. He was still mad about being so-near-yet-so-far from his hero.

"Did you want Mr. Paul to adopt you, or what? So you can be Baby Cannonball?"

"I'm not a baby!"

"Cannonball Junior?"

"I wanna see him fly! He's everywhere and we keep missing him!" Which was true, but how do you catch a cannonball?

After lunch, we walked down to the park office, where Melba had told us we could use the phone. She was doing paperwork at her desk while eating a tuna sandwich. "Hi, guys! Some party last night, huh?" She asked about Leo and mentioned being surprised that Pop was such a good dancer (she wasn't the only one). Finally, she got around to pushing the phone to the corner of her desk.

Mama answered on the first ring. The sound of her voice saying "Hello?"—bright and hopeful, like she knew it was us—flooded me with feeling. Maybe it was homesickness, or maybe just realizing how much I'd missed her. We started talking at once. She hadn't received any postcards yet, so I tried to give her the highlights: Big Brutus Dodge City camping out four-pound bass—"And guess what?" Gee shouted in the background. "I got a dog!"

I handed him the receiver and sat back, blinking fast. Melba went about her business, pretending not to pay any attention, while Gee got stuck on Cannonball Paul and couldn't get off.

"Did he say something about a dog?" Mama asked when I took back the phone.

"Well . . . we sorta picked one up." I didn't want to go into details just then.

"But your grandfather hates dogs! Is he okay with that?"

"Uh . . . more or less."

"How are you all getting along?"

"Fine. He's at work now." This made it sound like we got along best when Pop was fifty miles away, but oh well.

She started telling me about the number of chenille-wire wreaths and snowmen she'd racked up and how Lyddie came over the night before and helped her make pinecone trees and they had a blast except she missed us awfully. By then Gee was making like an inchworm trying to crawl up the side of Melba's desk, so I thought it might be time to wrap this up. "Well, Gee's getting a little antsy"—("I'm getting wormy!" he shouted)— "so we'd better go. Take care. Love you."

I got off the phone just as Melba was rescuing her pencil holder. "Is he like this all the time?" When I nodded, she said, "Your grandfather must be a saint."

If he's a saint, I thought to myself, *I'm an angel.* With pearly wings and a fourteen-karat-gold halo.

Pop returned early, as promised, with a bag of Ol' Roy dog food, a six-pack of Coke, and a lemon. "No dinner for me," he said. "You kids can fix what you want; tonight's my biannual liver flush."

I watched, unbelieving, as he poured half a cup of olive oil into half a can of lukewarm Coke, stirred in some lemon juice, and drank it.

"It'll take a few hours to work through the system," he said, for once not going into a lot of detail. "When it does, it's not pretty. This might be a good night for y'all both to sleep in the tent."

He took the time to run numbers with me on the laptop, then stretched out on the sofa with a book by somebody named Louis L'Amour and told us adios. So there we were, kicked out again. Some RV odyssey! Instead of reorganizing the cute little kitchen, I was building another wiener-roast fire in the great outdoors. Melba puttered up on her scooter. "Hi, Ronnie! Where's Jack?"

It looked to me like she'd touched up her makeup. "He's flushing his liver," I said politely.

Gee was trying to poke me with a peeled stick, like I was a hot dog. "He told us to stay out 'cause it won't be pretty!"

Melba thought this over. "I see," she said at last, then turned the scooter and puttered away.

"We might have shot a budding romance in the foot," I told Gee.

"Pow-pow!" he replied, pointing his stick down the road.

I was so bored, we tried roasting things besides hot dogs: bologna slices, baby carrots, Oreo cookies. Gee also tried teaching Leo to catch pieces of food in his mouth, but the dog responded the same way he had to all Gee's lessons: polite cluelessness. "So he's not only scared, he's stupid," I said.

"He's not stupid! His brain just doesn't work like other dogs'."

"I'll bet all doggie brains work the same."

"Don't either! Kid brains don't work all the same. Miss Puff says I'm differently abled."

Miss *Poff* was his second-grade teacher in Lee's Summit, whose name he never got right. "We're not talking about you, we're talking about—" I broke off at the sound of a vehicle coming our way—maybe another camper, which would at least give us something to look at.

But it was even better: a dusty blue-and-white pickup driven by Howard Sayles, pulling right up beside us with a smooth turn.

"Hey," he said, resting one elbow on the open window. "I had to bring Aunt Melba some garden peas, and she said y'all were up here by yourselves. You want to go for a little drive?"

Gee popped up like a spring. "I get to ride in the back! And Leo, too!"

I knew kids weren't allowed to ride in truck beds on the highway, but when Howard said "a little drive," he meant just that: "My aunt says only around the park. But that's a ways."

Leo balked at jumping into a strange pickup bed. When Gee said, "Come on, boy!" he just stood with his head cocked to one side, as though asking, *What is this 'Come on'?* When I spoke to him, he whined and slunk back. I suggested to Howard, "Maybe if you start off down the road he'll jump in anyway, like he did with the bike trailer."

Howard just stuck out his hand toward Leo. After a minute, the dog came close enough to sniff it. A minute later, he was standing still to have his ears scratched—like he'd never done for me. Howard patted the tailgate lightly. Leo crouched, then pushed off with his hind legs and landed on the bed, his claws sliding on steel.

"Cool!" Gee exclaimed, and pushed off with his hind legs, too.

Howard closed the tailgate while I ran over to pound

on the RV door and tell Pop where we were going. He yelled something in reply—probably "Okay," though I didn't stick around to make sure. Howard was in the cab, gunning the motor. When I jumped in, he shifted into reverse and backed away from the campsite. I said, "Hey, is there any chance you would let me drive a little?"

"Well . . ." He put the motor in forward gear. "It's a stick shift." I wasn't sure what he meant, until he shifted the stick down as we speeded up. "They're tricky to learn? Especially at night. If you're going to be here awhile, I might could come back in a couple days."

"Um . . . yeah." I just realized that this was my first time alone in a vehicle with a boy! Or not exactly alone—I turned around to check on Gee and saw two lumps sitting quietly in the truck bed, the smooth lump with one arm around the hairy one. Still, it was a weird feeling, and for the moment Howard seemed as tongue-tied as me. A mile spooled out under the wheels before he said, "Aunt Melba told me how you talked your grandpa into keeping the dog."

"Yeah, well, I didn't talk him into it, exactly. I made a bet with him."

"But you talked him into taking the bet."

"I guess." After a minute, I said, "The thing is, I can see Pop's side, kind of. Leo's been nothing but trouble so far, and even if we get him home we might not be able to keep him. Still . . ."

"Still what?" he prompted.

"I don't think any human ever took to my brother like that dog has. He's, like, the only one who'll put up with him no matter what. Of course, my mother and I do, but we have to."

"What about your dad?" he asked.

I hesitated, then told him about my dad. The truck lurched as he shifted down for climbing a hill. "Sorry," he said.

"That's okay." I knew the "sorry" wasn't for a rough transmission.

He paused at the top of the hill, then backed up. "This here's my favorite spot by the lake. Let's go sit outside."

He'd stopped at an overlook with a turnout and picnic shelters. We got out of the cab and walked around to climb into the pickup bed beside Gee. Not beside Leo, who backed into the corner when I came aboard, making like a spare tire.

"This is *neat*," Gee said happily. "The water has stars in it."

The lake nestled among the low hills like a mirror in a giant's palm. The wild Kansas wind had settled down to a light breeze that rippled the surface and made the stars look like they were jumping up and down.

"Ever' once in a while," Howard said, "the water's as still as glass. Except for when a fish strikes? Then it's like somebody stuck in a pin."

A turquoise band of sky wrapped the western horizon like a ribbon. Our voices sounded so quiet and cozy I wanted us to keep talking. "What do you do on the farm?" I asked him.

"Whatever needs doing. Plant. Disk. Cultivate."

"Cool!" bubbled Gee, who had no idea what two out of

three of those words meant (I wasn't too clear on them, either). "Do you have cows and horses?"

"Nope. My sister raises chickens. To eat? But we grow corn and soybeans."

"Do you drive a tractor?"

"Sure. Since I was five."

"Wow! I wish I was a farmer. Do you have to go to school?"

"Sure I go to school. We get out early sometimes, spring and fall."

"So you spend most of a day at school, then come home and work some more," I said.

"Yep." Howard's voice sounded matter-of-fact but proud underneath. "My folks'd have a hard time getting along without me." I thought about Mama getting along just fine without us, except for missing us, of course, and felt a touch of envy. "Look!" He pointed at the sky. "Shooting star! Did you see it?"

We both shook our heads.

"Keep looking, over there. See the Big Dipper?" I nodded, but Gee had to know what the Big Dipper was and pestered us until we'd traced it enough times to poke through the sky. "Watch that space between the Dipper and the horizon," Howard continued. "I'll bet we see some more."

We watched as the turquoise light faded to black and the stars came out thick as daisies. Gee was fidgeting when a silver scratch appeared in the dark sky, like an Etch A Sketch line. "I saw one!" we yelled together.

For the next few seconds, that neighborhood of the sky was full of them, as if it were the Fourth of July over there.

Gee leapt up and hopped all over the truck bed, making tools rattle and Leo cringe. "They're having a party!"

Howard told him to sit down, then asked, "Who is?"

"The angels. Maybe it's a bowling party, and the stars are bowling balls!"

"Sit down," Howard said again. Gee flopped on Leo, who groaned. "They're not really stars, y'know? They're meteors. Space is supposed to be full of meteors. Bombarding us all the time? But when they hit the earth's atmosphere, and start plowing through all those little particles? They burn up with friction. That's what you're looking at— There's another one." He leaned back on the side panel. "Sometimes you see lots of 'em. Depends on the angle they're coming from and how clear the night is."

I shivered, leaning back against the wheel well.

"You cold?" he asked.

"A little." The tank top and shorts I'd been wearing all day didn't cut it for night. He was pulling off the flannel shirt he wore over his T-shirt. "Oh, you don't have to—" Without a word he tossed it over to me, and it felt so warm I had to put it on. "Do you do this a lot? Come out to look at the stars?"

"Best show in town."

"Do they make you feel, you know—small?" In books and movies, people are always looking up at the stars and feeling like specks of nothing.

"Nope," he said, clamming up.

I pried him open again. "No? They're so big."

"Yeah . . ."

"There goes another one!" Gee yelled. "Whoosh!"

"I don't feel small just because they're so big," Howard said. "But because they're so awesome I feel . . . awed."

There was a long pause, while Gee made noises: "*Fzzzt! Yowza!*"

"So," I said at last, "you're not, like, blown away at all?" I was, with those billions of lights that looked close enough to breathe on me.

"Sure I am. That's what 'awe' is. What if God put 'em there to be awesome? Then I'm feeling just what I'm supposed to feel, right?"

"I guess. I'll have to think about it."

"In fact, it makes me feel kind of special. That I can look at 'em that way. You don't see ol' Leo wondering about the stars." He leaned forward and stuck his hand toward Leo, who stretched his nose out and sniffed before licking it.

"Maybe he thinks *you're* awesome," I said. I was thinking a lot more highly of the kind of boy who drove a pickup and wore a John Deere cap. Even if I didn't feel like licking his hand.

"*Zip-zip!* Two at the same time!" Gee flopped down between us to catch his breath. "It's like a hundred human cannonballs."

"Hey," Howard said, "you ever heard of Cannonball Paul?"

I'd have been happy to never hear that name again, but Gee was all over it. Howard had seen the blazing amazing Paul at the grand opening of Farm and Home World in Garden City. So Gee had to hear about his outfit (sparkly), what he said (not much), what the cannon looked like (uh . . . like a cannon, only really long), and how fast, high, and loud he flew. Howard thought it was pretty cool.

"Tell me about it," said I, sarcastically.

"I thought I just did. . . ."

"That's what I want to be when I grow up," Gee announced.

Howard laughed. "You'd be good at it, I think."

A bird piped up from the lake, starting a chorus of squawks and shrieks from its neighbors. "Sandhill crane," Howard said as Leo lifted his head and made a strangly whine. "Don't that dog know how to bark?"

Gee defended his mutt. "He was treated bad when he was a puppy. That's what we think. He's afraid of everything."

"That's no excuse. What's the point even being a dog if you don't bark?" Howard inched over to Leo—not so fast as to startle him—and made a low growl in his throat. The dog cocked his head, probably thinking, *What the heck . . . ?* Then Howard gave a sharp, low bark, and Leo wriggled back into the corner.

"Cool!" Gee exclaimed. "Barking class!" Next minute, we were running through the entire canine vocabulary, from *woof-woof* to *yap-yap* to *aroooooo!* Once Leo understood we wouldn't let him off the hook, he finally managed a yap that sounded like it had been squeezed through a rubber hose.

He was probably just telling us to cut it out, but Howard decided we'd made a good start. "Anyway, it's time for me to head for home."

After we'd motored around the lake and returned to our campground, I noticed another RV, bigger than ours, had taken up residence a few sites down. Howard stopped under the security light and let the motor idle.

"Well . . . ," I said. "Thanks for the ride and everything."

"Never thought I'd spend all that time teaching a dog to bark."

I laughed. "Next time, you can teach me to drive. Or we could go fishing again. I liked it."

"I like hooking a four-pound bass, too." He might have been making fun of me, but when he smiled, I didn't really care.

I put my hand on the latch and leaned against the door. "Well . . . good night."

"G'night," he said, and then: "Hey. You got an e-mail address or anything?"

Kent Clark says you should always have extra business cards on hand, so I reached into my shorts pocket and gave him one. He looked at it with respect, unlike my friends at school. "I've got to get me some of these."

"How about you?" I asked him. "I mean, do you have addresses and that kind of stuff?"

How *dumb* can anybody sound, I ask you? But he answered, with obvious pride, "Got a cell phone. Give me another card and I'll write the number." I passed one over, along with a pencil stub. After a few seconds, he handed them back, saying, "You ever need anything, just call."

That sounded so sweet it needed an appropriate reply. But just then my brother yanked open the door I was leaning on, and I fell out of the cab.

What came out of my mouth wasn't very appropriate.

This is a windy farm. I don't remember when we were there. They are kind of like whirligigs except for this. The whirligigs hang close to the ground and right next to my ears. They go clack-clack and drive me crazy. The windygigs are hugemongous and way over my head like stars. They drive me quiet.

Love, Gee Sparks

Mama—we miss you, too. xxx, R

Unfortunately, the worst things in life "just happen,"
too—there's no way you can plan for them.

—Veronica Sparks,
Olympic-caliber planner

The next day made me wonder why we'd ever left
Missouri. To begin with, I didn't sleep well in the tent with
Gee twitching and Leo snortling. After Pop left at dawn,
I dragged my sleeping bag inside and rolled up on the sofa.
When I finally rolled off the sofa, it was because Gee had
tied a bunch of empty tin cans to Leo's tail to see what he
would do. What he did was tear off like all his former abu-
sive owners were after him, which just made the noise
worse, which spooked him even more, and so on.

By the time we finally got him stopped, he'd turned over
an industrial-size garbage can and woke up the new neighbors, who were trying to sleep in. The lady of the house let
us know they'd come out to the lake for some peace and
quiet, and if we didn't tie up that dog *right now* she was
going to march down to the manager's office and complain.

"What were you thinking?" I hissed at my brother after
we'd freed Leo from the cans.

"I just wanted to see what would happen!" he wailed.

"Did you think it would be anything *good*? He was
traumatized when we got him—you probably set him back
a whole year. See? He's hiding again."

Leo had backed into his favorite spot between the rear wheels.

"I didn't mean to," Gee sniffed.

"Tell *him* that."

"Okay." He scooted under the RV beside the dog, and I heard him explaining, "I'm sorry, Leo, I didn't think it would scare you that bad. . . ."

Sighing, I went inside the RV to rustle up some corn-flakes. The milk in the refrigerator smelled a little on the sour side, which seemed funny because Pop had only bought it the night before. I poked a couple of Pop-Tarts in the toaster and turned on the radio but couldn't get anything besides country-and-western music and farm reports.

When the toaster popped, I decided to enjoy a nice quiet breakfast by myself. And after that, I'd straighten up the place—which definitely had a lived-in look by now, with my sleeping bag sprawled on the sofa and Pop's bunk unmade and his breakfast dishes in the sink. Maybe, if Leo could keep his boy occupied, I could even do a little orga-nizing around here.

No such luck, though. I was halfway through breakfast when Gee's scream came from the direction of the lake, where he wasn't supposed to be. Running down the nature trail, I almost got knocked over by Leo. Gee was right behind, his legs dotted with black slimy things.

We both freaked out a little—I can handle rampaging squirrels easier than black slimy things. "Where have you *been*?!"

"Down on the edge of the water," he wailed, "where the mud is."

That explained it—leeches. After we both stopped the *Eeeuuuwww* business, we discovered that the suction could be broken with a twig. Gee then figured out that they would attach to anything, and before I got them all off his legs he had one slurped onto each fingernail.

"That's disgusting!" I said. "They'll suck your blood."

"They won't suck my nails, will they?" He waved his black squishy fingertips in front of my nose.

"Get outta here! Why do you have to be so retard—?!" I stopped myself, but not soon enough.

"I'm *not* retarded!" He stamped with both feet, accidentally scraping his ankle on a piece of root sticking out of the ground, and had to walk the rest of the way home trailing blood. And it wasn't even noon yet.

For lunch we had string cheese and baby carrots and crackers, but no milk because it had gone so bad I threw it out. Then we walked down to the beach to kill the afternoon. After cooling off in the water, I buttered myself with sunscreen and stretched out on my beach towel. Meanwhile, Gee dog-paddled out to the guard rope and started thrashing around in the water like he was drowning. I paid no attention because he can swim like a fish—but a man who was building sand castles with his kids plunged into the water to rescue him. Only to find, when he got to the victim, that Gee was hanging on to the guard rope with both feet. The man dragged him back to the beach and gave us both a lecture on—guess what?—the Boy Who Cried Wolf. That story never sinks in with Gee, but the adult world doesn't give up.

I was really looking forward to Pop's return so I could

get a break—and when punching numbers into a laptop and cooking dinner looks like a break, that should tell you what kind of day I was having. So the sound of his Yamaha roaring up the road, earlier than expected, was music to my ears. Until I discovered it was only bringing him to wash up and change his clothes.

"Y'all can get your own dinner tonight," he said. "Here, I bought some more hot dogs."

"What—?" I sputtered. "Where are you going to be?" I wondered if he'd ever heard of "quality time," or if he just figured he'd already put in enough of that.

"Moderate your tone, young lady. Melba waved me down on the way in and invited me to her place for dinner." He disappeared into the itty-bitty bathroom.

I squared off against the door. "Is this what dancing the polka under the Japanese lanterns leads to?"

He didn't hear me with the water running, but in a minute he poked his head out. "Forgot to mention. We'll head out tomorrow."

"Where to?" I gasped.

"North."

That left me sputtering again. "But—but—"

He paused on his way to the shirt closet. "But what?"

"I'm . . . not ready to go yet." Lame, but I didn't feel like explaining that Howard had kind of promised to come by tomorrow and teach me how to drive a stick shift.

"Sorry, darlin'." Pop tossed me a preoccupied grin. "This *is* a business trip, you know. Wagon train's gotta roll." He frowned at his shirt rack. "What do you think? Polo or oxford?"

"Stuffed," I muttered under my breath.

"What's that?"

"Nothing. Pop? Could you maybe come back before dark and take Gee for a walk?"

"Huh?" He looked at me, the way he hadn't up to now.

"I could use a break, that's all."

"Oh," he said. "Okay, I could probably do that after we run the numbers for today. Now, how about some privacy?"

About ten minutes later, he left the RV, in clean khakis and a button-down shirt, trailing a scent of Old Spice. "Be good," he called, gunning his Yamaha.

Gee ran over with two handfuls of mud to give him a good-bye hug, but Pop scooted off just in time.

I dragged out the charcoal, remembering all the times in Kent Clark's book where he says to break out of your old routines. "Oh boy!" yelled Gee. "Can we roast marshmallows again?"

"We're out of 'em."

"Then let's roast Gummi Bears!"

"Why don't you go do something for a while, okay?"

What he did was enlarge the mud puddle he'd been working on and teach Leo how to make paw prints— mostly on the lower edge of the RV because it was so nice and white.

I decided that after roasting our hot dogs—which were getting *very* old-routinish—we'd take a nice long walk to the pay phone and call Mama. Melba told us earlier it was fixed. Since our neighbors kept giving us hostile looks, it seemed like a plan. Especially after the unopened soda can—the one Gee left too near the coals—overheated and blew up, spraying Coke everywhere. *"Cool!"* he yelled.

When we got to the phone, he was so sticky he'd caught a few flies. I dialed the number, and when Mama answered, he had to talk to her first. She finally got the full story of Leo in one piece—or rather, several pieces put together more or less in order: how he found us during a storm and we hid him for three days before I won him fair and square in a poker game, and Gee was having the most fun he'd ever had. Leo got a chance to talk to Mama, too, though he didn't have much to say until Gee pulled his ears.

When I got on, she sounded a little worried. "Is all that true?"

"Pretty much. If you factor out the Gee-ness."

She knew what I meant. "But do you mean to tell me your grandfather gets along with the dog?"

"He doesn't have to get along with the dog. The dog takes off like a shot every time Pop shows up." I told her about Leo's peculiar personality, which just worried her more.

"I'm not sure we can keep him. We'd have to get him checked out by a vet, and I don't have the money right now. . . ."

I had the phone cord stretched so I could keep an eye on my brother while he tried to get Leo to lick the flies off him. "Don't worry about it. This dog may ditch us before we ditch him."

"Is Gee behaving himself? Has he worn out Mad Mechanix yet?"

I ignored the first question. "Mad Mechanix? It's still in the original box, mint condition."

"What? You mean he's been staying busy without it?"

"That's one way to put it." I changed the subject. "How are you doing?"

"Really good, sweetie. Wait'll you see how much I've done. . . ." While she tallied up the snowman, stocking, and wreath count, I noticed that Gee was no longer in sight. I left the receiver for a minute, just to reassure myself. They—the dog and his boy, I mean—were crouched by the roadside, staring at the ground. Probably at the world's unluckiest earthworm. Back at the phone, Mama was raving about ". . . these darling little crocheted bells Lyddie found in a magazine. Wait till you see them."

"Cool."

"Ronnie? To tell you the truth, it's kind of bittersweet. I love having all this time for crafts, but I sure miss my munchkins. Still, I'm really proud of you—and your grand-father, too. I guess he's finally stepping up to the plate. Sounds like an experience Gee will never forget—"

Just then a high scream pierced the night—not Gee's. "He's not the only one," I said. "Listen, I'd better go see what he's up to. Talk to you later—bye!"

Gee was still by the road, only now he was on his feet, waving his arms like one of those whirligigs. Meanwhile, Leo was setting a new speed record for distance covered while dragging a nylon rope. But what really caught my attention was the lady standing next to a bicycle, scream-ing bloody murder while a man tried to calm her down. Melba came marching from her trailer across the road, while Pop stood at the open door with an expression I couldn't describe.

It took a while to sort everything out. When I'd seen Gee and Leo staring at the ground earlier, what they were looking at was a black snake with its long white belly turned up. Gee thought it was dead, but when he picked it up by the middle, it whipped around and tried to bite him on the hand. That startled him so much he threw it out into the road. Anybody would.

But in Gee's world, if he does what anybody would do, the results aren't what anybody would get. The place where he threw the snake happened to be occupied at that moment by a young couple on bicycles, out for a pleasant ride around the lake. She got hysterical, he ran his bike into hers, and the snake didn't come out so well, either. Let's just say he wasn't *pretending* to be dead anymore.

"I didn't mean it!" Gee bawled. "I didn't mean to!"

He might have been apologizing to the snake, for all we knew. But Melba assured the two cyclists that it was an unfortunate accident, and I made Gee say he was sorry. The man accepted his apology, but I wasn't sure the lady did. Anyway, they rode on.

Pop never budged from the trailer, leaving the parenting talk to Melba: "I hate to tell you, Gee, but this afternoon I got a complaint from a gentleman who was down at the beach when you swam out. . . ."

The lecture was for me, too, the gist being that I'd shirked my duty as brother's keeper. "But of course that's not all your fault. I've been telling your grandfather he shouldn't leave you alone so much, even though you're a very responsible girl. . . ." *Duh,* thought I—and who made him leave us alone tonight?

Before anything else could happen, I dragged Gee to the shower to scrub off the mud, exploded Coke, flies, gnats, and possible snake spit—even though it was still at least three hours from bedtime.

"Are we leaving tomorrow?" he called through the shower curtain.

"Sounds like it." I could have said more but restrained myself.

And that was just as well, because as it turned out, we weren't leaving tomorrow. Pop had everything packed up when we got back to our campsite, and the first thing he said was, "Let's go."

A dozen questions could have exploded out of me right then, mostly variations on *"Huh?"* But after taking a good look at Pop's face, I decided questions could wait. Even Gee decided that. He took his place at the dinette, and Leo hung around the bike trailer, ready to jump on when it started rolling. I was dousing the campfire when Melba rode up on her scooter. She'd brought half of a cheesecake wrapped in foil, and handed it over to Pop along with a few words.

Apparently, she'd given him an earful during their dinner for two; Pop's stony face didn't change even when she stood on tiptoe to peck him on the cheek. Then she gunned the little motor and swung away. Before hitting the road, though, she beckoned me over.

"Well, Ronnie, it's been fun. Good luck—" She stopped just short, I think, of adding, "You'll need it."

"Thanks."

She squeezed the handlebars, as though wondering whether to say what she finally said. "By the way, a couple of nights ago . . . in that third poker round? He had you beat."

"How's that?"

"He drew a full house, twos and fives. I saw it—maybe because he let me. But he folded instead of calling you."

I just blinked at her like a dork.

"I thought you should know." She smiled and kicked the scooter back. "Hope to see you again someday. Who knows? I'll tell Howard you said good-bye."

At the moment I wasn't saying anything, so she handled both sides of the good-bye for me as she waved and swerved the scooter.

It was a little after six when we left the state park and turned north at the first crossroads. We traveled awhile before I got up the nerve to ask, "Where are we going?"

He drove about a mile farther before answering, "Chalk Pyramids. To set up a met mast." Then, after a minute, "Please tell your brother to stop kicking the dinette seat. I can feel it from here."

I went back to communicate the message and stayed to play rock-paper-scissors until Gee got bored and sleepy. Then I returned to my seat and pulled the map from the door pocket. The highway we were on headed north as straight as a needle. I followed it past Scott City, not sure if Chalk Pyramids was a town (black letters) or an attraction (red letters). Then it jumped out at me, on its tiny red-letter feet: CHALK PYRAMIDS, next to MONUMENT ROCK, both represented by red squares surrounded by white, at the end of a double-line track that meant a dirt road. Something about it, stuck at the end of that hollow road, hit my chest with an empty feeling.

But that was nothing compared to the feeling I got when we actually saw the place.

CHAPTER 12

Even the worst experiences can teach you something.
Learn the lesson!

—Kent Clark,
preaching again

By the time we'd turned off the highway and bumped and shuddered up a long dirt road, the sun was sitting on the horizon like the yolk of a fresh egg right after you break it in the skillet. "Twenty after eight," Pop read off the dashboard clock. "Should have about half an hour till dark. I'll set up my stuff. Then, with any luck, we'll get to the next campground by ten."

When the driver's door slammed, Gee woke up. He'd been asleep for the last half hour or so, his head rolling against the back of the dinette seat in a way that made my neck sore just looking at it. "Where are we?" he yawned.

"Chalk Pyramids."

He unbuckled his seat belt and came forward, squinting through the windshield. "*Those* aren't pyramids."

What he meant was, they weren't big triangles with camels and palm trees around the base. They were like Egyptian pyramids might look if you held them up to a fun-house mirror—stretched-out, lopsided structures bitten by the wind.

"Awesome!" Gee breathed in my ear. That was a good way to put it—as in Awe. Some. As in, not-quite-part-of-this-world.

Leo was already whining by the door because our grandfather had kicked him off the trailer in order to get at the equipment in the storage garage. I could hear Pop rummaging back there.

"Go ahead and run around," I told Gee, "but don't go anywhere near *him*." Usually when I say "run around" that's what he does—or even if I don't. But after hopping out the RV door, he just stood there, hugging Leo, as if he'd slammed into an invisible wall.

If you were a Martian, you might have felt right at home. In the pinkish glow of twilight, it looked like another planet, where they built houses from plans drawn by Dr. Seuss. The colors were all reds, browns, and grays, with some pale green mixed in. When I walked all the way clear of the RV, the west wind hit me with a sandy sting. That's what made the pyramids—years of wind and sand playing around with the rock. Now it was playing around with me—if I stood here long enough, I'd become a pillar of sand myself.

It made me hungry for company, even Pop's. He had found a spot on the other side of a column to set up his met mast. When I reached him, he was running out lines to stabilize it, while the weather vane on top spun like the Tasmanian Devil. "Come over and hold this steady for me," he commanded. "The ground is hard as a rock."

I took hold of the mast while he screwed a stake into the stony soil, then attached a stabilizer line to it. "Isn't this, like, public property?"

"Yeah. Got a permit to set up a temporary station."

"But nobody's going to build a wind farm here, are they?"

"It's for comparison." He strapped a boxy instrument the size of his hand to the mast.

"What's that?" I asked.

"Anemometer. Measures wind speed."

Since he was talking, however little, I sprung the question that was bugging me. "What's your hurry, Pop? I mean, why'd you change your plans so you could do this tonight?"

"Well." He took a paper from his pocket, slipped it into a plastic sleeve, and fastened it to the post. "That is—" He gave the pole a shake to test it. "All of a sudden, tonight seemed better than tomorrow."

That was a non-answer, but it confirmed what I'd already figured out on the way here. He was going to rush the second half of his assignment in order to get rid of us sooner. The original plan was to spend a few days in southwest Kansas, a few days in northwest Kansas, and a day or two somewhere in between. Then we'd retrace the whole route to get another set of readings before heading back to Missouri. But Pop could come up with a Plan B as well as I could. He was hurrying what he had to do out here, and then Gee and I were homeward bound—I was pretty sure.

"Go round up the herd," Pop said then. "Time to hit the road."

To affirmatize my attitude, I tried on the idea of going home sooner than expected. Big hugs from Mama, finishing my closet project, calling up this girl Marie that I'd started to make friends with and asking her if she'd like to go to the pool some afternoon. Sure it was old routine, but after all, routines were important for getting things done.

Gee's counselors were always telling us how he needed to be on a schedule.

But still . . . going home early was admitting to failure. I mentally ran through my short-term goals for this trip:

Learn to organize better. Are you kidding? What made me think Gee on wheels was easier to organize around than Gee at home?

Build relationship with Pop. So maybe he wasn't mentor material, but every time we started to build *something,* Gee would smash it.

See new places. Okay, but there was a lot we'd missed—what about the Wizard of Oz Museum and the World's Largest Ball of Twine?

Get away from old places. Exactly—and I wasn't ready to go back.

I started down the slope with an angry snort that Pop didn't appear to notice. Gee had loosened up enough to start a game of hide-and-seek with Leo around the boulders, but when I called, they both trotted over like cooperative little lambs.

Pop climbed into the cab and buckled himself in, then turned the key in the ignition.

The motor kind of burped. Then it didn't do anything.

The ignition clicked as Pop turned it off, then on again. "The battery can't be dead. It's brand-new."

I didn't know much about internal-combustion engines, but this didn't sound good. "Are we out of gas?"

He didn't answer but popped the hood and yanked open his door. "Did something fall out?" Gee called after him. Pop didn't answer that question, either.

For about ten minutes, he either stared at the motor or trudged back and forth from the storage garage, muttering a little louder with each trip. Then he jerked open the door and hiked himself up on the seat.

His lips looked too tight for talk. Then he said, "I think the alternator's shot." A few more seconds passed, while I held up a warning finger for Gee to zip his lip. "The warning light must not be working. I'm sure I would've seen it."

"What's an alternator?" I asked, very quietly.

"Starts the battery. If it goes bad, the whole electrical system is kaput."

I thought about the sour milk that morning and wondered if the electrical system was already kaput-ing back then.

"I'll take the bike and go get one," Pop said. "Y'all can stay here."

"Wh-what?" My voice didn't come out right at all—it sounded about eight years younger than me. Maybe because I felt like a scared little kid just then.

"You'll be fine. Just make up your beds and go to sleep. I'll be back before you know it."

"But why can't you wait until tomorrow? There won't even be anything open now!"

"And while you're gone we could be attacked by bears!" Gee protested. "Or lions!"

Pop made an effort to hold on to his temper. "Look. Once I get back on the highway it's only about sixty miles to the interstate. There's a truck plaza right at the exit that's open all the time—I'll be back in two or three hours, install the alternator, and we're good to go. If I wait until tomorrow, it's a whole day's work gone."

How does that compare to a boy and girl gone? I wanted to ask. Not that I really thought we'd be eaten by lions, or anything like that, but still . . . this place was so big and empty I could almost feel it swallowing me.

"Furthermore, Gee, there aren't any bears or lions out here." Pop was using an exaggerated let's-be-reasonable tone of voice. "Nothing will get you if you just stay inside."

All that did, of course, was reinforce Gee's idea that there might be something *outside* to get us. He continued to protest—bringing up tigers in addition to the other wild animals—but of course it didn't do any good. As soon as Pop had unloaded his bike and reminded us about staying inside, he took off in a flurry of dust. We watched the little taillight all the way to the point where the horizon gulped it down. The dark closed around us.

"We're all alone!" Gee wailed.

"No we're not," I said, desperately looking for positives, even while the aloneness boomed all around us as big as the wind. "Leo's here to protect us, right, Leo?"

At the sound of his name, the dog—who'd been cowering under the rear axle—crept out, whimpering.

Gee clutched him like he'd never let go. "He's scared, too."

"Then maybe you can protect *him*."

"We don't like this place."

That makes three of us, I could have said. In the sunset it was kind of neat and spooky, but now it was just spooky, period. The light of a quarter-moon and a slew of stars made the chalky columns rear over us like black ruins—the hideout of mummies and zombies in every scary movie I wished I'd never seen. I shivered, and it wasn't just because the temperature had dropped. "We'd better go inside."

Gee begged to bring Leo, but I wouldn't allow it. To tell the truth, I was mad at everybody: Pop for leaving us here, Gee for cutting short our trip, and Leo for being a dog—which wasn't fair, I'll admit, but Leo had certainly helped push Pop to the limit.

"Inside" didn't seem much better than out after I switched on the overhead light and got only a weak, eye-straining glow that seemed worse than nothing. "Oh yeah. Our electricity's gone." That meant no radio to keep us company; even farm reports would have sounded like music just then. I turned off the switch and reached for the flashlight. "Let's find our jammies and go to bed."

"*No!*" he protested, exactly like he was three years old and afraid of missing something good if he went to bed. Seriously, I wouldn't have minded missing the next few hours. "I won't go to bed without—without a shower!"

This was a new one. "But you already had a shower, back at—"

I was interrupted by Leo, who was crouching just out-side the door. He let loose with such an odd noise—between a moan and a yap—we both stopped to listen. Out of the silence came a sound I couldn't describe. It was more like a police siren than anything—a lot of police sirens. Just when I started wondering if the cops were coming to tell us Pop had been wiped out on the highway, the noise broke up into sharp little yips. Leo scratched at the door, whining.

I said, "No telling what he's scared of now."

"I know!" Gee exclaimed suddenly. "It's coyotes. I heard 'em at the campout last fall."

His Sunday-school teacher took the boys on an overnight to Smithville Lake, which wasn't quite overnight for Gee when he fell out of a tree and cracked his head. "Are you sure?"

"Wouldn't you be sure about a noise like that?"

Sometimes he makes sense. "Are they, like . . . dangerous?"

"My teacher said they were scared of humans. But—"

"Let's just stay inside."

"But Leo's out there! You said I had to protect him!"

Me and my big fat mouth. It led to a big fat argument: Gee's side was that we either let Leo in, or let Gee out. My side was that when Pop found dog hair on his cushions we'd be heading home a lot sooner, maybe on the first eastbound truck. Besides, I was tired of bending over backward for a mutt who could probably take care of himself. The fight went on while Leo scratched at the door, making every noise a dog could make that wasn't a real bark.

Gee finally won, with a pretty good tactic: he stopped breathing.

Not exactly on purpose; it was his asthma kicking in. His attacks are getting fewer and farther between, which is the upside. The downside is that they're scarier when they happen. First he starts choking, next his eyes get big and

round, and finally these ugly noises like a rusty saw start
coming from his throat. By then Mama is telling him to
stay calm while she looks for the inhaler, and if she doesn't
find it fast enough his lips turn blue. So now I was looking
for the inhaler, and not remembering where I put it.

"Just stay calm," I kept saying. "Sit down and concentrate, okay? In . . . out . . . I know it's here, I remember
packing it—"

Trying not to panic, I turned over the sofa cushions
and rattled through the closet shelf and every kitchen cup-
board. The flashlight beam darted like a terrified mouse—
"In! . . . Out! . . . That's good!"—while his raspy breath
was sawing my nerves apart.

I even climbed up to Pop's bunk and checked the storage bins there, screeching when a stack of books spilled on
my toes. One of them caught my eye because it didn't have
a cowboy on it; barely believing my eyes, I read, *Seize the
Way*. . . . Pop was a Kent Clark fan, too!

But no time to wonder about that. "Hold on—we're
getting close!" We'd better be, because I was running out of
places to look.

"Leo . . . ," Gee croaked, feebly waving toward the
door.

I decided that desperate times called for disobeying
your grandparent. Jumping off the bunk, I opened the
door. Leo bounded in, Gee slid off the dinette seat, and
they met in the middle of the floor. Dog hair wasn't exactly
good for asthma. But Gee was still breathing—or gasping—
so I figured Leo's love outweighed his allergens.

The inhaler was under the dinette seat. I snatched it up and checked the batteries and plugged it into Gee almost before he could get his next gasp. Then we all settled down like flurried leaves drifting back to earth. Leo was panting like a big old machine of dogginess, I was taking long deep breaths, and Gee was sucking on his tube while the hiss of the inhaler filled a space that had never felt so tiny before now.

Meanwhile, the coyotes were carrying on outside like a maniacs' convention. The wind was making a low, steady moan that rattled the thin walls. "Make up your beds and go to sleep," Pop had said. Sure.

The RV felt just the opposite of safe. It felt more like a pressure cooker that was slowly filling with the inhaler hiss and every thump of Leo's tail—which, whatever comfort Gee found in it, was probably stirring up even more dust and dander. My flashlight picked up the gleam of Gee's eyes, which didn't look any less scared than before. *Thump. Thump. Thump.*

"All right, here's what we do," I said. "We'll build a fire."

Gee blew the tube out of his mouth. "In *here?*"

"Of course not! While we were outside a while ago, I saw a little rock circle on the other side of the RV where somebody built a fire. There's even some wood left. It'll scare the coyotes away and be a signal for Pop when he comes back." The thought crossed my mind that maybe Pop wasn't coming back, but that just shows what being alone on the Kansas prairie at night will do to your thinking.

I found some matches and a blanket and herded Gee and Leo out of the RV. Whoever had built the last fire in that spot had even left a pile of papers for kindling—about twenty sheets held down by a rock. They looked all the same, like some kind of advertising flyer. Gee sat on a blanket nearby with Leo tucked around him like a rug, while I wadded up some of the paper flyers and rearranged the half-burned logs and twigs in a tepee on top. Three matches made the paper blaze and the wood crackle, sending sparks into the air.

"Cool," Gee breathed. "Fireworks."

"It's just cinders from the paper."

"No, I mean in the sky. Look!" I turned on my heels, just in time to see a couple of shooting stars. Two more showed up right after, and for a couple of minutes the sky was full of them. We watched, holding still as though we were afraid they would notice us.

Gee spoke up, in a trembly voice. " 'Member what Howard said? How they're heading for us but the angels bat 'em back before they can hit us?"

That's not at all what Howard said, but I couldn't help picturing a heavenly host with baseball bats, whapping away into deep space. The idea wasn't too far-fetched—if they were stuck with this guardian-angel gig, why shouldn't they have some fun with it? We watched for a while, keeping score and feeling less alone. The universe looks friendlier when you can see it as part of one big game.

"I guess they're looking out for us," I said, in what was

meant to be a reassuring tone. The wind gusted, making the flames twist.

Gee worried, "Maybe it'll blow out like a candle."

"No—see how much brighter the fire gets when the wind blows? Air's like food to a fire. Hey, how about we write another postcard? We still have the sunflower one left."

"What's that?" The wind had carried off my stack of unburned paper, and Gee jumped up to chase them.

"Come back here!" I yelled. "You'll get your asthma going again!"

After a minute, he raced back, with a fistful of papers and Leo at his heels. "Look what I found!"

"It's just some kindling left over from the last person who—"

"No, look!" Since he was waving the papers right under my nose, I couldn't see anything until I snatched one sheet out of his hand and tilted it toward the fire. It was an advertisement with a photocopied picture that looked all pebbly. The words read:

Coming soon to Hays, Kansas!

Special engagement!

Don't miss the blazing, amazing, spectacular

CANNONBALL PAUL!!

Ellis County Fair, June 14–15 . . .

"He was here!" Gee shouted, jumping up and down.
"Right here!"

I had to admit, that was the likeliest explanation. Who else would have enough Cannonball Paul flyers to burn but Cannonball Paul himself?

And why did we keep following him, like rats behind the Pied Piper?

This. Was getting. Too. Weird.

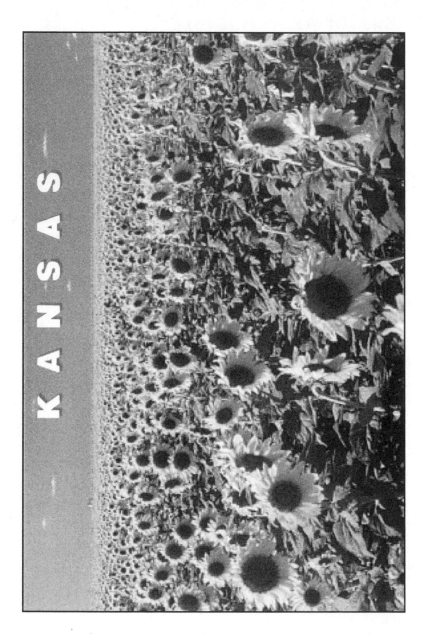

KANSAS

This is a sunflower farm but that's not what I want to tell you.

We are chasing Cannonball Paul. He's this guy in a silver suit and a golden head who shoots himself like a bullet. He looks like I feel. I mean, I wish I could feel. I want to see him so bad my stomach hurts right now. The wind is blowing really hard out here. I'm filling up with sky. My cheeks swell up and my eyes push out and Ronnie says I'm running out of room. I just want to catch Cannonball Paul. And that's all.

M—some imagination, huh? We're fine, see you soon, R.

CHAPTER 14

Some downsides just stay down for a while.

—Veronica Sparks,
who knows what she's talking about
(unlike some bestselling authors she could name)

The sound of a lone motorcycle puttering up a gravel road at two-fifteen a.m. can be more beautiful than a fifty-string symphony orchestra—at least if you know who's on the motorcycle. The wind had died down and the night was so clear I could hear Pop's Yamaha while it was miles away; at least twenty minutes went by before the headlight finally came in view. It was just me and the coyotes awake by then, because Gee had sacked out on a doggie-pillow by the fire (with pictures of Cannonball Paul clutched to his chest and blazing, amazing visions dancing in his head). Leo woke up long enough to creep under the axle.

I had stayed awake to keep the fire going, but Pop didn't say anything about that, or anything about the late hour except, "Took longer than I thought." I'd noticed that. He grabbed a shovel from the storage garage and helped me smother the fire, then unsnapped a bungee cord, untying a square box from his fender rack. "I'm going in for a few hours of shut-eye. I'll try to get this thing installed at dawn. Then we'll see where we are."

I knew where I was: out in the middle of nowhere with a next of kin who didn't even bother to ask "How'd you manage out here all by yourself?" Or say "Sorry for taking

so long," or "Good night," even. I gave him a couple of
minutes to get settled, then dragged Gee inside. Just before
crashing on the sofa, I tucked our latest postcard into the
mail rack, little suspecting I would never get a chance to
mail it.

What woke me up, in the pinky dawn, was Pop banging on
the motor. I tried to guess by the speed and loudness of the
bangs whether his mood had improved any, but they didn't
tell me much. When I got up to wash my face, the weak
dribble from the faucet warned me that our water had
almost gone the way of the electricity. If this alternator
thingy didn't work, we'd be stuck out here with the rocks
and the sagebrush until some tourist with a lot of time on
his hands happened by.

I opened the passenger door and hopped to the
ground, pausing by the rearview mirror. The hood was up,
making a crack I could see through without being seen.
Pop didn't look too bad. That furrowed brow and down-
turned mouth probably just meant heavy concentration.
He tapped with a hammer and turned a couple of screws
with a socket wrench. Then he reached into the motor and
gave a sharp tug. The engine turned over so loud and sudden I jumped. When he slammed the hood, his mouth was
still turned down, but his eyes looked a lot more cheerful.
"I'll let it run for fifteen minutes to charge up the battery,"
he told me. "Then we're outta here."

That's not exactly how it happened, though, because
Gee woke up with his own agenda. "Are we fixed? Are we
on the road?"

"As soon as Pop loads his bike," I told him. "And Leo might like to be fed, so—"

"Pop!" Gee bounced out of the RV, trailing the blanket I'd tucked around him. "Pop! We have to do something!"

One thing for sure: our grandfather was in no mood to be told what to do. I dashed out behind Gee, too late—he was already hopping from foot to foot and waving pieces of Cannonball Paul in front of Pop while the latter was trying to load his bike onto the trailer. ". . . and he was already here, maybe just before us. He's following us! No, I mean we're following *him*. Look: he's gonna be at this place called Hay. We have to find him, we just have to—"

I grabbed him by the arm, hissing, "Not now! We can bring this up at—"

"Po-op!" Gee wailed. Our grandfather had managed to keep his temper, wrestling a two-hundred-pound bike while a very annoying kid waved papers in front of his face. Now he snapped around with his hands up, waved them as though batting away flies, and stomped between us, headed for the cab.

"Did you understand the body language?" I said. "Let's just get on board and shut up."

"But I didn't feed Leo!"

There was no time now to unpack the dog food, so we tossed a Pop-Tart into the trailer. Leo sniffed at it, probably wondering why they didn't make a bone-marrow flavor.

For the half hour that it took to get off a gravel road that didn't know when to quit, Gee sniffled and whined. Pop's knuckles, gripping the wheel, turned whiter and whiter. Finally, I unbuckled my seat belt and slipped back to the dinette table to lay it on the line: "He's just about ready to stop this vehicle and throw you out. And if you don't stop the whining, I'll open the door for him. Suck it up and deal." Not too sympathetic, maybe, but I wasn't feeling much sympathy at the time. And it shut him up, which was my primary goal.

Later on, I wondered if more sensitivity could have changed the unfortunate direction events were soon to take, but who knows.

Pop finally came to the end of the gravel, and we turned north, bidding a fond farewell to the Chalk Pyramids. We'd gotten an early start, just like he wanted. A bleary-eyed sun was swimming up through the haze that promised our first really hot day. It didn't promise much else, though; another lonely campground with not much to do except ride herd on Gee & Leo, Inc. My attitude was about six feet under by then, flat on its back with a rock on its stomach, and for once I didn't care one bit.

That's when Gee screamed, and Pop gasped, and the RV swerved off the road.

Once we were stopped, Pop's temper finally snapped. He started pounding on the steering wheel: "Don't you ever, *ever* do that again!"

Gee was pointing straight ahead, at a billboard on the right side of the road advertising the Ellis County Fair. Featuring—did you guess?—Cannonball Paul in his shiny suit with the golden helmet tucked under one arm.

"There he is!" Gee pointed out the obvious. "There he is! Are we going that way? Pul-eeease?"

Pop was gripping the wheel. I could feel the exasperation

in him—no, on second thought, I could feel the *rage* in him, building up to a big crescendo, like the place in the movie where the building explodes or the stalker leaps out of hiding. Only this crescendo was *totally* silent. Which is even scarier, in a way. The feeling rose to the point where I was sure we were toast, but then it started going down. Without the explosion. I thought that was a positive sign until he said, in an almost-normal voice, "We are now."

He started the ignition again and eased onto the road so carefully you'd think we were in Chicago during rush hour instead of so far in the boonies that another car would be an event, almost.

Gee said, "We are? Oh boy!"

He's not what you'd call sensitive to nuance. But I knew something wasn't right. Once we were on the road, I carefully asked, "Um . . . what do you mean, Pop?"

"I mean this is it. The last straw. The point of no return. In other words, I'm taking you home. Right now."

I spun around to glare at Gee. But he was gazing back at that stupid billboard, which quickly shrank to the size of a postcard, then a stamp, before disappearing altogether. Then he turned around and said, "Can we stop at Hay on the way?"

I would have screamed, except we were going over a bridge just then, and if Pop lost it we might end up at the bottom of a ravine. So I took a breath and said, "Pop, you don't mean that."

"I beg to differ, Ronnie." He seemed perfectly calm now, the worst sign yet because it told me he'd made up his mind and was fully comfortable with the decision.

"You'll lose a whole day's work! And you won't have me to help you run numbers."

"More like two days' work. But I'll make it up easily after a little side trip to Missouri. And thanks to your excellent assistance in getting me set up—which I appreciate—I'm capable of punching in numbers for myself. Now please explain the situation to your brother in any way he understands."

I heaved a huge sigh, snapped off my seat belt, and hurled myself to the little-brother situation room (meaning the dinette table). "Okay," I told him, "vacation's over. As of now we're headed home—you know, little house on Maple Street, Mama on the couch—"

He just blinked at me. "Uh-huh."

This was not the response I expected. "So . . . try to keep quiet until we get there. Did you know we have Mad Mechanix? In this very vehicle?"

"How far is Hay?"

I grabbed the tail end of my temper. "First of all, it's *Hays,* not Hay. Second of all, don't even bring it up, okay? Just let it go. It won't take much to shove Pop over the edge, and if he goes he might take us with him."

"Uh-huh. But how far is it?"

I keeled over on the dinette seat and put a pillow over my head, feeling like a gerbil on a treadmill. What was the point of even trying to reason with him? Our budding relationship with Pop was wrecked and our vacation cut short, for what? A seven-year-old's obsession with a guy in a golden helmet. If I hadn't dozed off from lack of sleep, I would have steamed myself into a red-hot tamale by the next stop.

When I woke up, feeling no better, Pop was steering the Coachman onto the asphalt surface of a huge truck plaza. The place was like a little city, with three restaurants and two repair shops, an auto-parts store, and roughly a hundred vehicles breaking every rule in the driver's-ed manual. Nearby, the interstate thundered with traffic—I hadn't seen so much action since we left Missouri. When the RV had dodged a few semis and pulled up in front of a gas pump, Pop turned off the motor and made an announcement.

"First I'm going to fill the tank. Then I'm going to find the restroom and wash up like I haven't had the chance to do since night before last. Then I will call your mother. And finally we'll start for home. Headed due east on I-70, I figure we'll be there before suppertime."

This was when the news finally sank in with Gee. "We can't go home!" he yelled. He unbuckled his seat belt and hurled himself at Pop. "*Please!* We haven't seen Cannonball Paul yet!"

Pop tightened his lips, like I'd seen him do a lot lately, unwrapped Gee's arms like they were tentacles, and marched him back to me with a look that told me this was my problem. After he left, I said, "Forget about Paul, okay? It's not going to happen."

"It *has* to happen!"

I drummed my fingers on the table, trying to think how to distract him. "When we get home, I'll go to the library and look him up on the Internet. He's bound to

have a Web site with his schedule. So when he comes anywhere close to us, we'll go see him, I promise."

"What's today?"

I counted up days on my fingers. "It's the thirteenth."

"*June* thirteenth?"

"Duh. Of course."

"He's in Hay tomorrow. I'll bet he's going there right
now—where is it? Show me the map."

I yanked the map out of the door pocket and showed
him where we were in relation to Hays.

"It's only a *inch*," he protested.

"More like seventy miles—"

"Just one more day? Please?"

I wadded up the map and threw it into the sink. What
was the point in trying to organize anything if your little
brother always blew in like a Kansas tornado and tore your
plans to shreds? "Get this through your thick brain—we
are *not* going to Hays! We are going home, and it's all
because of you, screwing up my life as usual!"

He balled up one fist, but didn't let fly—smart enough
to know I'd pop him back if he did. So he stamped his foot
and yelled, "I don't care! I'm going to Hay!" He ran to the
door, threw it open, and jumped out.

Next minute, his red T-shirt disappeared behind a corner of the convenience store. *Good riddance,* was my first
thought. Leo had jumped off the trailer, but with all the
cars and trucks and noise he got no farther than the nearest pump island. There, he turned a few circles as though
looking for a scent, then slinked back and crouched next to

the right back wheel, debating whether to crawl under or not.

I grabbed a piece of Melba's cheesecake from the fridge for something to chew on. Besides nails. Pop was still fueling, calm as a pond, and for all his face showed, he'd never even heard of such a thing as "grandchildren." My heels slammed against the storage bin under my seat, harder and harder, as though trying to make a dent. Finally, Pop topped off the fuel tank, replaced the nozzle, and stuck his head inside. "You want anything?"

A nice, normal family, I thought. *A real vacation—and how about some control over my life?*

But he was talking about convenience stores. Sighing, I pulled myself up and went to fulfill my mission in life: managing my little brother.

Gee wasn't in the main building. I searched the convenience store, the taco stand, the pizza stop, even the full-service sit-down restaurant, but no sign of him. The other side of the building was the truck port, a maze of roaring semis and towering trailers.

Circling around outside to the cars and minivans, I noticed that Pop had moved the RV to a parking lot beside the store and locked it. Leo whimpered at me from the trailer as though asking where Gee was. "Go find him yourself," I snapped, but of course he wouldn't venture beyond the nearest curb.

By the time I'd scouted the store again, the worry weasel was starting to creep up on me. Pop was in the restroom—maybe Gee was there, too. Not knowing what else to do, I hung near the door marked GENTLEMEN, waiting for one or both of them to come out. The two

waiting for one or both of them to come out. The two restrooms faced each other, making a short passageway to the back entrance and the big glass doors leading to the truck port. A pay phone was nearby, plus a couple of newspaper stands and a rack with brochures about local attractions. Of course Cannonball Paul was there, next-to-last on the third row. I was reading headlines at the newsstand, when the reflection of a vehicle on the glass made me turn around.

For a couple of seconds, I couldn't believe it. Rolling by just outside the glass doors was a big white trailer with gold letters: BLAZING, AMAZING, and you know the rest.

The trailer was already past me. Hardly thinking, I pushed open the glass doors and shouted, "Hey!"

The driver didn't hear or see me, and the vehicle was already rolling so fast I couldn't catch up, even while running and shouting "Hey!" like a total maniac. And even if I could catch up, what would be the point—to ask for his autograph, or if he'd pretty-please stuff my brother into his cannon? It was only after I stopped, watching the truck hit the highway and head for the interstate ramp, that the thought hit me—

What if Gee had found that trailer and stuffed *himself* in the cannon? What if he was at this minute being carried away by none other than Cannonball Paul?

Four wheels don't make a friend, but they can sure help.

—Veronica Sparks

I ran back inside, hoping my crazy idea was wrong and Gee would be playing dodgeball with the ice dispenser or demolition derby with soup cans. Something normal, at least for him. But no—I checked down every aisle and behind every revolving book and CD rack without catching even a glimpse of him.

Then back out the front door. Leo had crept off the trailer and was sniffing around the tires. When he caught sight of me, he let loose with one of his strangled yelps. He swung in the direction of the highway and yelped again, then hopped up on the trailer and turned around to look at me. There was something on his mind, for sure. Could it be something like, *My boy is in the big white rolling box and we need to go after him right now?*

After a few seconds, he went through the whole pantomime again, and I was convinced. Rushing back through the store, I found Pop at the pay phone with calling card in hand, getting ready to punch in our home number. "Wait!" I gasped. "Don't do it yet!"

He lowered the card and stared at me.

"Gee's gone. I mean, really gone. Here's what I think—"

"What I think," Pop said, "is that he's outside climbing a pole, or else he's hiding from us, for spite."

I just shook my head. Gee didn't do anything from spite; that took too much thinking. But when I went on to tell Pop my suspicions, he refused to believe a seven-year-old boy would be bold enough to stow away in a stranger's vehicle.

I made a big effort to keep both feet on the floor and speak quietly, ticking points off my fingers the way Pop did. "Number one: Paul doesn't seem like a stranger after Gee's been obsessing over him all week and sleeping with that promotion card under his pillow. And number two, boldness doesn't have a thing to do with it. He just does stuff without thinking, or maybe he thinks by doing. I've never figured that out. Whatever—" This became point three: "It's like when he climbed up the side of Big Brutus. He wasn't being brave or showing off—he was just doing what was in his head right then. See?"

Pop moved the receiver toward the phone, then back toward his ear, then hung up. "Well, maybe."

"Pop! He's getting farther away from us every *second*."

"All right," he said abruptly. "When was this guy supposed to be in Hays?"

"Tomorrow."

"That means he'll be camping there tonight. I'll get the bike and go to Hays and check it out. You'd better stay here."

"Stay here?!"

"In case Gee turns up. Don't get too far from the pay phone. I'll take this number along and call as soon as I know anything."

That was the plan and he was sticking to it. I followed him out to the RV and suggested we ought to call the police, but he didn't think much of the idea. "And tell them what? That we think Gee sneaked into a cannon? We can handle this without the establishment, Ronnie."

This was his contrariness showing, though I had to admit, as he roared off on the Yamaha, he looked up to handling anything. Still, if one Gee-seeker was good, five or six more would be that much better. I turned it over in my mind while searching the store and the restaurant and the parking lot twice—then the question was taken out of my hands.

"Did you lose something, honey?" asked the store clerk while I stood near the magazine rack looking a little lost myself.

BECKI, read her name tag. She looked so sympathetic I couldn't hold back. "Yes, ma'am—my little brother." As I explained the situation, her eyes got wider and wider, and when I got to the part about my grandfather not calling the police, they bugged right out.

"If that's not just like a man! I never heard of such a stubborn—of all the—don't you worry, honey, I'm calling the highway patrol this minute."

Not only that, but after getting more details from me, she put out an Amber Alert right there in the store, just by raising her voice: "We have a missing child—a boy seven years old with light brown hair, wearing cutoffs and a red T-shirt. Please report if you have seen this child." Then she turned on the outside speaker and repeated the announcement. Everybody was looking around as though they expected to see my brother behind the potato-chip bags or under their front axle. It was all pretty intense until a

Kansas Highway Patrol car arrived, then people started quietly paying for their gas and slipping away. The authorities would take care of it.

Within the hour, four troopers in three cars turned up, meaning I had to repeat the whole story to each one. All of them seemed skeptical that Gee would do what I was sure he did. Plain old kidnapping was more along their line, but if they knew my brother they'd understand that any kidnapper would think twice before nabbing him. At least Officer Hadley, the first one to appear, got on his radio with a fellow patrolman in Hays and asked him to track down Cannonball Paul.

While this was going on, I heard the pay phone ringing and almost knocked down a little girl while rushing to answer it.

Pop's voice sounded thin against the road noises in the background. "I'm right outside of Hays. Just got here— thought I'd call and make sure Gee hasn't turned up. I guess he hasn't."

"No, but—"

"I'm going to head to the fairgrounds and see if that guy's checked in yet."

"Pop, I—"

"There's too much noise here. I'll call back later. So long."

The phone clicked in my ear before I could tell him to expect a patrol car or two. The troopers were discussing strategy outside, so that's where I went to share the latest news: "My grandfather is at Hays. He's going out to the fairgrounds."

They told me they'd put out an Amber Alert for my brother so that every police officer, convenience-store clerk, and gas-station attendant in Kansas would be watching for the aforementioned seven-year-old with light brown hair, brown eyes, and a red T-shirt. Somehow this didn't make me feel one bit better.

Don't get me wrong—Amber Alerts are terrific and avert many a tragedy, I'm sure. But this was *Gee.* This was my brother. None of your ordinary kidnap scenarios seemed to apply.

I wandered back through the store, where Becki was telling every customer to be on the lookout for a seven-year-old boy with light brown hair, et cetera. In the back lobby I collapsed on a bench between the pay phone and the brochure racks, trying to remember what Kent Clark said about dealing with a crisis.

He wrote a whole chapter about Advantaging Your Anxiety, but "anxiety," to him, seems to mean stuff like losing a pile of money from a bad investment or having the transmission in your Lexus fall out—not misplacing a family member who's accidentally almost killed himself lots of times. My Anxiety squatted like a big concrete garden toad on my chest, so heavy I could hardly breathe. Where was the advantage in that?

Not that I thought Cannonball Paul was dangerous— or was he? I pulled one of his cards from the brochure rack and stared hard at it, as if studying his face would give me a clue to his character.

The silver suit and golden helmet kind of screamed for your attention, so you didn't notice much about the face.

But that might be because there wasn't much to notice. He was young, or at least not old, with blond hair combed straight back from a face that was not gorgeous but hardly ugly. The most striking thing about him was the pose: feet apart and chin up, one hand on his hip. Like, CAPTAIN AMERICA SAVES THE WORLD.

Just sitting here was going to drive me nuts. I took the phone book off its shelf under the pay phone and looked up "Hays, City of." There were listings for the fire department, the collector, the police, the mayor . . . some of which might be useful. I reached in the pocket of my shorts for my ever-ready pencil stub and felt one of my business cards. It was the one with Howard's cell phone number on it.

My hands were shaking, but after a couple of tries on the pay phone I managed to punch in all the calling-card numbers, plus the cell-phone number. Then I listened for the ring with my heart pounding in my ears.

After five rings, and my heart almost giving up, I heard a click. Then a voice: "Hey."

"Howard?" My own voice sounded like it was climbing a pole, but I got the squeak under control and spilled out the whole story: hasty departure from the campground, Chalk Pyramids, Cannonball trailer, highway patrolmen. The order was a little mixed up, but he seemed to get most of it. A few seconds passed before he asked, "Where did you say you were?"

I told him. After a few more seconds, he said, "You're not gonna believe this, but I'm only about forty minutes away. Had to deliver some hay to a ranch in Rush County."

"Where's that?"

"Where I'm taking the hay? Over by the Barbed Wire Museum."

Barbed Wire Museum? Only in Kansas. "Howard—can you come?"

He could have asked, *What for?* I wasn't sure how to answer in a way that made sense, but what I really wanted was to do something besides wrestle a stone toad—namely, go to Hays and look for Gee myself. Howard had the wheels. But did he have the will?

"Sure," he said.

By now most of the patrolmen were gone, but Officer Hadley came in to say good-bye for now and to pat me on the shoulder. "Just stay put so we can reach you. And don't worry. Becki said she'd look after you, and we've got the whole state looking for your brother." I just nodded, my mind about fifty miles away.

During the next half hour—the longest half hour of my life—the store manager brought me a Coke and a plate of nachos, and Becki sat with me during her break. I was too jumpy to appreciate it. Finally, I hinted around that I could use some quiet time, and they more or less left me alone.

When the blue-and-white pickup finally pulled up in front of the glass doors, it looked as beautiful as a limousine. I gave it a *just a minute* wave and dashed back to the counter.

Becki was checking out a customer, still giving her description of Gee like she knew the poor little boy. I snuck up on the opposite side of her and slipped one of my cards halfway under the register. It read: *Left with a friend. Call 555–7890* [Howard's number] *if you have info.*

In the lobby I paused to make sure no one was looking, then darted out the doors and hopped in the truck. "Thanks," I gasped. Howard nodded at me and gunned the accelerator. As we roared past the RV lot, I shouted, "Wait!"—almost hitting the windshield when Howard hit the brakes. "We'd better take Leo."

"Right." Howard pounded on the side of the truck cab. "Hey, Leo! Come on, boy!" With no hesitation, the dog leapt off the bike trailer and bounded over, clearing the tailgate with a mighty bound. When he was settled, thumping his tail so hard the back window rattled, Howard shifted gears and pulled out of the lot. "Which way?"

I pointed to the right and he turned the wheel, joining a line of vehicles waiting at the stoplight. Directly ahead, I-70 hummed with cars and semis. "Oh, man," Howard said.

"What?"

"I forgot about the interstate. I'm not used to . . ."

"Used to *what*?" I practically shouted.

"Traffic," he said as the light turned.

Stay calm, I told myself. "Howard? It's green." He moved forward, but so slowly the driver in the SUV behind us gave a blast on the horn. "Look, no sweat. My dad was a truck driver. The interstate was his office. Seriously. He was always complaining about bad drivers on ramps and how it's supposed to be done. So I can talk you through it. Come on, let's do this. How about a right-turn signal . . . Good, but give it some gas."

Biting his lip, he turned onto the entrance ramp and nervously tapped the accelerator. Up we went, slowly drawing level with the semis that roared by so fast they created their own wind tunnels. I'll admit, trucks had never looked so big and mean before. "Don't look behind you!" I told Howard. "I'll watch back here, just keep your eyes on the road. Turn signal . . . No, *left* turn signal."

"I knew that," he said quickly.

"Don't slow down! Just keep steady. . . . You're doing good." *Whoosh!* A cattle truck whizzed by so close the pickup wobbled. "Okay, now speed up—no, *don't!*" The SUV passed us with another angry honk. "Same to you, guy! Now it's clear. Step on it, Howard. STEP ON IT!"

He stomped the accelerator and nudged over into the right lane, wincing as another huge tractor rig buzzed his left. "You *did* it!" I squealed, bouncing on the seat. "Now we just go with the flow."

His hands were still gripping the wheel too hard. "Wait'll I tell my folks. No, on second thought, maybe I'd better not."

"What *did* you tell your folks?"

"The truth. Well, enough of it. Told 'em something came up and I had to give a ride to a friend."

"They trust you to take off like that, without knowing who the friend is?"

"Sure." The tone of his voice made the question sound kind of silly. If he ever screwed up really bad, like losing his little brother at a truck stop, his parents' attitude might change. But for now, I didn't mind him being Mr. Perfect.

Howard pushed the old truck up to sixty miles per hour before speaking again. "One time last spring? My little sister got lost in a Wal-Mart store in Scott City. Got away from my mom while Tyler and me were playing

Carnivore's Castle in the electronics. We looked all over that store. Inside and out. Store manager made an announcement and all that. Somebody in the lawn and garden found her asleep. Behind the compost bags."

"Well, that's nice," I said after a pause.

"All I mean is. Almost all these cases turn out okay. Thousands of kids get lost every year. . . ."

"And most of them get found," I finished for him.

"Yeah." I knew we were both thinking of the ones who didn't.

By now it was about one p.m. on a bright sunny day, and up ahead of us the highway disappeared. I'd noticed this in the Coachman: you can see the asphalt in front of the hood, and feel it rumbling under the wheels. But farther ahead, whole patches of road seem to shimmer and vanish. They were like huge puddles of . . . nothing. It's freaky—you know it's a mirage but still can't help wondering if the next few hundred yards are going to be there when you reach them. When I'd noticed this before, the wondering was kind of a game. Now it was anything but.

My eyelids were getting too heavy to prop open. The steady hum of wheels pulled me down into a rumbling, gritty state that some might call "sleep."

"Hey," Howard said. "You awake?" I sat up in time to see the HAYS CITY LIMIT sign flash by. "We'll need directions to the fairground—"

"Over there." I pointed to a green sign with white letters: ELLIS COUNTY FAIRGROUNDS/NEXT RIGHT.

"Got it." Howard took the exit (getting off was a lot

easier than getting on) and turned at the first left. Two more signs showed us the way after that, and before long we were on a quiet two-lane road with a water ditch down one side and more trees than I'd seen together since we left Melba's campground.

"How far *is* it to this place?" I was getting ready to leap out of the window with impatience, when I heard a tapping sound.

It was a scratching, really, made by Leo's claws as he swiped at the glass. I'd almost forgotten about him.

"What's up with that dog?" I exclaimed as Howard slowed the truck to a crawl and looked over his shoulder. With the engine noise cut back, we could hear Leo whine for our attention. When he had it, he backed up a few feet and almost-barked.

"What do you think that means?" I asked Howard.

"I think we'd better have a look." Shifting in reverse, he backed up slowly while Leo turned circles in the truck bed. Suddenly, he lunged at the tailgate.

"Stop!" I had my hand on the door latch, popping it open when Howard hit the brakes. Jumping out of the cab, I ran to the spot where the glint of wheel spokes had caught my eye.

Sprawled at the bottom of the ditch was my grandfather, his face under the helmet as pale as dust.

People are like boxes of Cracker Jacks—
there's always a surprise inside.

—Veronica Sparks

For a moment, I couldn't move. Mr. Clark can say what he wants about expecting the unexpected, but this was too much. Howard scrambled down to get a closer look. "Is he dead?" I yelled.

"No," he answered, and the word felt like a Swedish massage on my gnarled-up nerves.

I made my own way down the slope. It made me a little queasy to see blood soaking Pop's jeans from a nasty-looking cut on his leg, but even worse was how helpless he looked: unconscious, with his Adam's apple sticking up like a shark's fin from his stretched-out neck. I put a couple of trembling fingers against the place where a vein was twitching. "Feels regular, I think. He doesn't seem to be in shock." I wasn't sure what "in shock" looked like, but first-aid manuals always mention that accident victims should have their feet elevated, if possible, so blood can flow to the head and un-shock them. Pop was already lying that way—his blood should have been flowing like the Mississippi.

"Don't move anything," Howard said. "I'll get my phone and call an ambulance. You stay here and watch him—"

Like I would go anywhere? While he climbed back up to the road, I felt around in my pockets for something to fan with, and came up with a Cannonball Paul postcard. "First help you've been," I muttered to the picture, fanning hard at the base of the helmet so the air could get to Pop's face. I saw his Adam's apple bob. Then he sneezed—not a little achoo, but a great big honking *ahhhh-CHOO* that made the helmet bounce. While I stared at him, he reached up and pulled it off, then lay there blinking at me.

"What are you doing here?"

Nice greeting, but that's Pop for you. While I flapped my lips trying to come up with an answer, he bent his elbows on the ground, like he was intending to sit up.

"No, don't!" I cried. "You might break—"

He just sat up anyhow, favoring his right side and making faces like he was being tortured. Howard skidded down the slope, with his phone in one hand and a Kansas map in the other, stopping himself so short he almost tumbled over on us. "Whoa! You're not—I mean—should you be sitting up, Mr. Hazeltine?"

"I'm sitting, aren't I?" No just-call-me-Jack small talk now.

"Pop, what happened?"

"Durn rock on the road. I must have been dozier than I thought or else I would have seen it. Front wheel slewed, I lost control, ended up—well, you see."

Howard spread his map on the grass. "I'm fixing to call 911. Where are we?"

"Don't bother with an ambulance. All I am is sore. I just need a minute to get back on my feet."

"Pop—" I began.

"Mr. Hazeltine, you could have internal injuries you

don't know about. You could be bleeding like a stuck pig inside. One time my uncle turned his tractor over and—"

"Spare me the cautionary tales." Pop bent his knees, steadied his two feet under him and his left hand behind him, and rose bit by bit. It seemed to go fine until he wobbled, and put out his right hand to grab my shoulder, and made a noise halfway between a groan and a scream. Leo, who was still on the bank looking down on us like an anxious mama, pricked up his ears and whimpered.

"What's wrong?" I gasped.

"Sharp pain—here." Pop was gasping, too, one hand on his left side.

"Might be a rib broken." Howard probably didn't mean to sound this way, but there was a definite a-*ha* tone in his voice. "That's what happened to my uncle. You'd better get an X-ray, at least—"

"All *right*. But put away the phone. We can get there quicker in your truck." Pop was already on the way, climbing the slope with his right arm out for balance.

Howard fiddled with his cell phone, as though tempted to call 911 anyway, but I just shook my head. "You don't know how stubborn he is."

"Hey." Pop was almost at the top of the slope when he turned around. "Can y'all bring up my bike?"

It wasn't a big monster Harley, just a medium-weight, buzz-around Yamaha, but try dragging one uphill sometime. Howard took a lot more than his share—"This is nothing, next to horsing hay bales around"—but even he was puffing pretty hard when it came to hoisting the thing into the truck bed.

Leo was pacing the width of the bed, and I could almost swear he grinned at the sight of his old traveling buddy. The bike, I mean, not Pop.

We had to backtrack a couple of miles to a convenience store where we could ask directions, but soon we were on our way to relief—for Pop, anyway. He sat between us in the cab, wincing with every bump. Leo trotted from one side of the pickup bed to the other, making the rear end sway like a hula dancer's hips.

"What's the matter with that mutt?" Pop grumbled.

"It's a good thing we had him along," I told him. "He's the one who saw you in the ditch and made us stop."

Pop turned his head in my direction, but his neck was so stiff he couldn't turn it far. "Will wonders never cease," he said—and the funny thing was, he didn't sound sarcastic at all.

At the Ellis County Hospital, the emergency-room hustle and bustle was just like when Mama went in for her knee. Funny to think that happened only two weeks ago. The cut on Pop's leg had to be sewn up, and the X-ray showed hairline fractures on two ribs. Not too bad, the ER doc admitted, but he still insisted on consulting a specialist about possible internal injuries. Pop was fully alert through it all, and able to answer all those next-of-kin questions himself. When they asked him about insurance, he just took a wad of cash out of his wallet and slapped it down on the desk. "Who needs insurance?"

My eyes bugged out—my grandpa was *loaded*.

After he was bandaged up, we all sat in the waiting

room while the specialist was supposed to be looking at Pop's X-rays. The lull only reminded us of our bigger problem, that Gee was still missing. When Howard's cell phone rang, all three of us jumped. He fumbled it out of his shirt pocket, finally answering, "Hey?" Then he said, "Hold on, sir," and moved the phone away from his mouth. "It's the highway patrol."

"Oh yeah," I said. "I didn't get a chance to tell you, Pop, but the clerk back at the truck stop called them, and—"

Pop took the phone, with a grimace-y look at me, and for the next few minutes we heard, "Yes . . . No . . . Uh-huh . . . Right . . ." All the good stuff was on the other end of the conversation. But then he said, "I don't know about that. . . . I understand, but . . . Well, as to that, here's the person you should talk to." With no further warning, he stuck the phone at me.

I took a breath. "Um . . . hello?"

The voice on the other end sounded frazzled. "Who's this?" I told him. "Oh. Ronnie, this is Officer Hadley. I'm the one who talked to you at Trucker's Rest." After my assurance that I remembered him well, he went on to say that they'd really expected me to stay put so they could reach me easily, but since I didn't—

"I'm sorry," I said, hoping to speed this up a little.

"Well, anyway, I'm at the county fairgrounds, where I just talked to Mr. Dominic."

"Excuse me?"

"Better known as Cannonball Paul," he said impatiently. While I blinked in surprise that a human cannonball even had a last name, Officer Hadley went on to say that

Mr. Dominic was astounded to hear he was a kidnapping suspect, and more than willing to have his trailer searched. The patrolman admitted that Paul could have been hiding Gee elsewhere. But he, Officer Hadley, had been in this business a long time and knew all the standard ways people acted when they were trying to cover up, and Mr. Dominic seemed like the real deal. So—

I'd been trying to break in for the last three sentences at least. "But . . . But, sir . . . Just a minute . . ." Finally, silence at the other end. "What I'm trying to say is, I don't think Gee was kidnapped. He volunteered."

After a pause, the patrolman said, "Yeah, you told us. Frankly, it's a little hard to believe, and even if he did stow away on that trailer, I don't know how we could have missed him. Officer Garcia and I went through every conceivable hiding place."

I could have told him about the time Gee squirreled himself away in the wheel well of our dad's truck when he was only two, but didn't want to get sidetracked. So while he went on about the unlikelihood of the thing, I stood up and paced all the way to the opposite side of the waiting room, trying to think what to do now. "Anyway," the patrolman was saying, "I just called to let you know. How long can you be reached at this number?"

Howard was tilting his chair against the wall with his arms folded. I made a guess: "Um . . . at least until six."

"Okay, let me give you my number. Got a pencil?" After taking the number down, I walked back to return the phone.

Pop was sitting one seat over from Howard, with my

empty chair between them, and as I came nearer he looked more and more like a stranger. *Old,* for one thing—still kind of gray in the face, with sagging shoulders and a something in his eyes that the pain left there. It made me feel kind of responsible. At the beginning of this trip, it seemed like he owed us, like he had some grandfatherly dues. Mama sure thought so. But maybe the credit balance was more on his side now.

I gave the phone back to Howard and sat down, trying to think what to say to Pop. "Uh . . . I hope you know . . . Gee's not a bad kid, it's just—"

"He's like me," said my grandfather.

"Huh?"

"I was just like that, only my family wasn't so long-suffering. That's why I spent two years at the Collins County Boys' Home."

"The . . . Collins County . . ."

"Reform school."

"Whoa," Howard said under his breath, just before getting up to visit the men's room or whatever.

Kent Clark has a whole chapter on Conceptualizing Conflicts: it's about how to understand where people are coming from so you can work with or around them. But this floored me. What did Pop do to get stuck in a reform school? And did he get all the way reformed? I had to ask: "Are you, like, an ex-con?"

He sighed. "Here's the story. At twelve I accepted stolen merchandise my best friend cadged from a hardware store. At thirteen I robbed the hardware store myself. At fourteen I stole a car and drove it into a telephone pole. That's when my folks gave up and the court took over."

"Does Mama know about this?" I was wondering if she'd have let us go on a road trip with him if she had.

"Look, Ronnie, I learned my lesson. Crime doesn't pay. So I got my life straightened out and stayed out of trouble, and there was never any reason to bother your mother about it."

So why bother *me* about it? He must have been more shook up than I'd thought. "Pop . . . if you knew what Gee was like—because that's what you were like—then why did you turn your RV around that day and come back to Partly for us?"

He didn't say anything for the longest time. Then, slowly, he reached around to his back pocket and pulled out a square of folded paper. Unfolded, it turned out to be a piece of light blue construction paper with a picture drawn in colored felt-tip markers.

Even though Mama and I could write the book on felt-tip markers and what happens when they get into the wrong hands, I had to admit it was a cute picture: a house with windows and a chimney, with smoke coming out of the chimney in a pig's-tail curl. Just the way every kid draws a house, except this one was on wheels and had a box stuck on one side that looked a little like a truck cab. Inside the box was a grinning face with a cowboy hat.

Stapled to the upper corner was a typewritten note from Gee's Vacation Bible School teacher at Partly Baptist Church. The note said, "Dear parent, Today in our discussion time we talked about our families. Each child in the

class drew a member of his or her family and shared what
that person meant to him or her. We helped each child
think of one thing they appreciated about that family
member, and give thanks for him or her. Your child
wanted you to have this."

Under the vehicle was printed, "My Pop is strong and
loud and chases wind. He drives a big shiny truck. He won
it being a hard body. When I grow up I want to be like
him. Thank you God. Love, Gee Sparks." The printing
was so neat I knew somebody else wrote it, but *Gee Sparks*
was in my brother's own hand.

Pop said, "I found this on my bunk, that first night
after I left your house."

And it melted his frosty heart. The funny thing is, all
this time I thought he'd softened up and come back for us
in spite of Gee. But no—it was *because* of Gee.

Expect the unexpected.

I looked up to see a nurse standing in front of us with
a clipboard, saying, "Mr. Hazeltine, Dr. Achmed thinks it
would be wise for you to check in for some tests—"

"Tests," Pop repeated. "What kind? Spelling tests? IQ
tests?"

Her smile twisted to one side. "In accidents like this,
there's often internal bleeding or fractures that the
victim—"

"The only bleeding I'm concerned about right now is
in my bank account."

Everybody in the waiting room was staring at us. I
grabbed his sleeve and tugged on it, like I do when Gee's
acting up.

"Mr. Hazeltine," the nurse began in a low voice, "I don't think you appreciate the ramifications of . . ."

Pop turned his face halfway toward me and winked—seriously, even though it was only a little tip of an eyelid. Then he murmured, "Go get the truck."

I took off as Pop raised his voice to say, "I appreciate how much a Band-Aid goes for around here, not to mention a test. Now, what did you bloodsuckers do with my *hat?*"

I turned a corner and ran into Howard, who was studying the contents of a vending machine. "We're outta here," I panted.

Less than five minutes later, we pulled up to the ER entrance, and there was Pop, hat in hand.

CHAPTER
17

The wind blows where it wills.

—God

By the time we got to the fairgrounds, it was almost five o'clock and the fair was in full swing. "Where's the campground?" Pop asked the first orange-vested parking attendant we met, and the next, and the next. Being volunteers from the local 4-11 or whatever, none of them knew. Howard had to drive all the way to the gate before we found a guy with OFFICIAL STAFF on his cap. The smell of barbecue and corn dogs hit with gale force, reminding us that we were starving, but nobody suggested we stop for a snack.

Following Mr. Official Staff's directions, Howard drove halfway around the fairground and took a side road that dipped into gullies and made our teeth rattle. Soon we found ourselves in familiar territory—a loop of narrow asphalt road surrounding a shower house, toilets, and drinking fountains—but instead of retired couples with motor homes, these campers hauled huge livestock trailers and trucks with logos on the doors. "'Happy Times Carnivals,'" Howard read under his breath as he drove slowly past. "'Angus Farms . . . Eat It and Weep Bloomin' Onions?'"

"Over there!" I pointed at the spot on the farthest end of the loop, where a very familiar white trailer was parked under a spreading oak tree.

The pickup coughed as we pulled up, motor racing a

little when Howard turned it off. Pop opened the cab door and eased himself out. "Let me handle this." We watched him limp up to the trailer and knock on the side door, then wait. And knock and wait again.

I got out and let down the tailgate for Leo, who hit the ground and headed straight for the trailer as though on the scent. But once he reached it, he seemed confused, turning circles and trotting from one end to the other, whining.

"Has this dog ever been good for anything?" Pop said, knocking for the third time. I could have reminded him how Leo found him in a ditch that very day, but at the moment the dog wasn't scoring any points with me, either.

"Hey there!" came a voice from the road. "Are you-all looking for Cannonball Paul?"

We turned as one, to see a short white-haired lady in pink polyester slacks and a smock. She went on, "He left a little while ago in his truck. I saw him while I was on my evening walk."

Pop lowered his knuckles, and I asked her, "Do you have any idea where he went?"

"None in the world," she said cheerily. As she came closer, I could see that the pattern on her smock was all onions—the bloomin'-onion lady, maybe. "Are you related to that little boy who's lost?"

Wow—Gee was famous. Pop's expression turned grim as he nodded.

The onion lady nodded back sympathetically. "Paul couldn't have had anything to do with that—he's a real nice young man. But don't worry. Those state troopers are on the job. They spent two hours here this afternoon—why, the whole place was in an uproar."

"When will Paul be back?" I broke in, before she could describe the uproar.

"Now, now, I'm not his appointment secretary. Here comes his brother—why don't you ask him?"

That gave us all a start; Paul had a brother? Somehow I'd gotten the idea, maybe because of all the Captain America–style pictures, that human cannonballing was a solitary occupation. The onion lady pointed down the road, where a young guy in shorts and sneakers and nothing else jogged toward us. He was all shiny with sweat, which told me he'd been running awhile, but when we called to him he just waved a hand and chugged on by.

"Hey!" Pop shouted again, but the runner either didn't hear or didn't want to break stride. Pop looked at me, and I took the hint.

The last year we were in Lee's Summit I went out for track, but by now I was way out of shape. Catching up with him was easy, but this conversation would have to be quick because my endurance stank. "Hi, Mr.—uh—I'm Veronica Sparks."

"Hi," he said, on the beat. "Tim."

"Why I'm here." I was already starting to pant. "It's my brother who's lost."

"Right. We don't have him."

"Not on purpose, but—I mean—he's got this huge crush on your brother—I mean, on the whole cannonball thing—and—"

"Regulate," he said.

"Huh?"

"Your breathing. Three beats in, three out." He demon-strated, drawing long, healthy breaths. "Or three in, two out if you need more oxygen." However long he'd been running, he didn't even seem winded. Not a big guy, but he had an upper body that wouldn't quit.

"Okay." I breathed in for three beats. "My brother—is hiding around here—somewhere. That is—I'm almost positive. We need to ask Paul—if he'd let our dog—sniff around the trailer."

"Looks like that's what he was doing," Tim remarked.

"I mean—inside the trailer." Two in! Two out!

"Sorry. We don't let anybody in there."

"Not even—the highway patrol?"

"Oh yeah. Paul was pretty ticked about that."

"When's he coming back?" I gasped.

"In time for the exhibition shoot, around seven."

"What's—an exhibition—?"

"Kind of a teaser. We load the cannon with a dummy and shoot it over a power line. Or something. It flops around like a wild man. People who weren't planning to come to the fair on Friday decide they have to come any-way and see the real shoot. Fair committee likes it—sells more tickets."

"Ah—" I was about to drop dead. "Could we talk to Paul—like—after—the shoot?"

"Sure." He reached into his shorts pocket and pulled out a wallet. Never breaking stride, he opened it and took out some slips of blue paper. "Passes. We always get 'em. Never have anybody to give 'em to."

"Thanks." That was my last word. I fell back, and Tim waved before swerving onto a path that led into the trees.

I stumbled back to the trailer, where Howard and Pop were looking for traces of Gee. Leo was sniffing busily but not ecstatically, as I was sure he would have if he'd picked up a real scent.

"He's not here," Pop told me grimly. "We've been calling his name and nobody answers."

Howard nodded toward Leo. "The dog won't give up, though. I think maybe Gee *was* here. Scent's not strong enough to get Leo excited? But he's sure interested."

Breathily I told them what Tim said about the exhibition shoot. Howard perked up. "Hey, maybe Gee'll show up for that."

Pop snorted. "Right. They'll be ready to shoot *him* out of the cannon by then."

An idea struck me. "What if he's at the fair right now?" They looked at me, Pop skeptically, Howard with that gaze that was so wide open a monster truck could drive through it. "Look," I went on, "all he wants is to see Paul fly. What if he heard something about the exhibition shoot—maybe without understanding it was a dummy going to get shot, not Paul—and decided to hide out long enough to see that. Then after, he could just walk up to the nearest official-looking person and turn himself in and go home. He'd be ready to go home by then. It's not like he's running away— he's running *to*."

Pop frowned. "Could he . . . *concentrate* long enough to carry out a plan like that?"

Good question. "I don't know."

"Well," Howard suggested after a pause. "We ought to mosey over and see what we can see. And maybe get a barbecue sandwich."

"Oh yeah," I said, remembering. "It won't cost us anything, Pop—Paul's brother gave me some passes."

Pop just snorted. "I'd pay our way in. What kind of tightwad do you think I am?"

He did shell out for the barbecue, even for Howard, who was low on funds. Howard used the dinner break to call home—which he had to do from a pay phone because he'd let the battery on his cell run down. From his side of the conversation, it seemed his mother was having some trust issues. "Uh-huh, Hays . . . Sorry, I thought I told you that. . . . Well sure, the interstate's the fastest way to get there. . . . I know my license is restricted, but this was an emergency. . . . No, it wasn't a problem. . . . Yes, ma'am, I know, but . . . but . . . I can't come home now because—"

Eventually Pop took the phone and convinced her that Howard really was helping out friends in need—especially since he was the only transportation we had now. After promising that he'd take care of their boy, Pop hung up the receiver and said, "Let's split up. Ronnie, you can search the midway. I'll take the exhibit halls and Howard the livestock barns. Meet back here at six-thirty, and if none of us have Gee, we'll find out where this exhibition shoot is."

Howard took Leo, mainly because he was the only one the dog would willingly follow. I started down the midway feeling reenergized from the food, but after almost an hour of peering behind carnival rides and under ticket booths and getting yelled at by barkers wanting me to try my luck, I was exhausted all over again. A tall dark bank of clouds had piled up while I wasn't looking. The wind picked up, turning chilly. I shivered, wondering if the exhibition shoot would get rained out—and then what?

All of a sudden I was back where I'd started, at the midway entrance. Exhausted, I dropped down on a bench beside an old man in overalls and a snap-brim hat who seemed to be taking a nap. The sky had grown so dark that the midway lights had turned on. Carnival booths were flashing a gaudy, steady *toc–toc–toc* that almost hypnotized me. Announcements from the speakers, pops from the shooting gallery, and tunes from three different rides were fighting for my attention; the competition was giving me a headache. The Tilt-A-Whirl made me dizzy, the Ferris wheel made me woozy, and the pirate ship made me seasick. The barbecue wasn't setting too well on my stomach, either.

A hard gust of wind blasted us with sudden cold. People stopped and looked up as a slow roll of thunder muttered across the sky. Somebody said they'd heard a tornado watch was in effect. Any minute now, the midway would shut down, and Paul would call off the exhibition and Gee might stay in hiding and who knew what would happen then?

I tried to drum up a pep talk from Kent Clark about silver linings, but the wind suddenly balled itself up and hit the fairgrounds with a punch that sent food wrappers and silly hats flying—not to mention all those catchy phrases about supersizing your life. "Whoooo!" everybody said, looking up again.

The man beside me on the bench reached up to make sure his hat was still on his head. Then he kind of shook himself, like a dog waking up, and looked over at me. "The wind bloweth where it wills, and thou canst not tell whence it comes nor whither it goes." He nodded at me with a little smile, then stood up, brushed off his overalls, and strolled away.

Whatever, I thought. Then I noticed it was twenty after six.

Pop was already waiting, Gee-less, at our meeting spot, and the look on his face when I trotted up, also Gee-less, told me he was pretty worried. Maybe even more than I was. "I don't know what to do after this," he told me, echoing my own thoughts. Even though it was partly the wind that made his voice sound funny, there was something else in it, too.

Without thinking, I took his hand and squeezed it, and his other hand kind of found my shoulder and pulled it toward him, and soon we were clinging together like orphans in a storm.

That's how we were when Howard turned up. "Hey! Cannonball Paul's in the livestock arena right now! The shoot got moved up 'cause of the weather—come on!" A voice crackled over the loudspeaker, announcing the time change.

We joined a stream of people headed that way. "Where's Leo?" I hollered, to be heard over the noise.

"He's under the stands. Tied him up. So I could come get ya'll? He'll stay put—all the people make him nervous."

Sure enough, when we got to the arena that scaredy-cat canine was cowering under the stands, trying to ignore the dog-lovers who stuck their hands under his nose. The speakers were playing some big, brassy military number, with cannons firing in the percussion section. Or that's what it sounded like.

The scene in the arena burst like a firecracker on me.

On one end was a net, like a soccer goal, only lots bigger. Smack in the middle stood a tower, about sixty feet high, probably made for bungee jumping or rappelling. The tower was the tallest thing in sight, but all eyes were elsewhere: the big square platform draped with red, white, and blue. On the platform was a huge tube, so white under the lights it was blinding—the famous cannon, of course. And in front of the cannon stood Cannonball Paul himself.

We'd come here to see him. I'd been expecting to see him, just like this or pretty close, and still he took my breath away. After staring at pictures of him all week, it was like a fairy tale coming true. In that silver suit—and yes, with the gold helmet tucked under his arm—he made my eyes hurt.

The cannon looked long enough to hold him, but not wide enough. One end of it was punched with regular round holes—for exhaust, I guess—and the other end pointed up toward the tower. Paul was pointing, too, and talking, but the words that came out of the loudspeakers were buzzy and the background music smudged them up even more: something about how he designed the cannon with a secret process that was known to him alone. Tonight we would see the stupendous effect, but if we came back tomorrow at one p.m., it wouldn't be a dummy flying over the tower to land in the net, but Paul himself.

Then the music shifted to a long drumroll as he picked up a life-size crash-test dummy and hoisted it to the mouth of the cannon. There, it disappeared—as if the mouth had slurped it right up.

The wind shifted, blowing a puff of cool, damp air in our faces. Thunder rolled slowly across the sky again like a million-pound bowling ball; lightning pulsed behind the clouds that were now directly overhead. "Gee's got to be here somewhere," I said, tearing my eyes away from Cannonball Paul. "If he's not . . ." Like Pop, I wouldn't know what to do if Gee wasn't here. It would be like the road disappearing in front of my eyes, dropping into a nightmare of the unknown.

"What's up with Leo?" Howard asked.

The dog had crept out from under the stands and was straining at the leash. His nose twitched, tasting the wind now blowing our way. Noises started coming from his throat: first whimpers, then whines. Howard untied the leash and held it as Leo lunged to the bar that separated the stands from the sawdust. "I wonder if—" he began.

"Maybe he smells—" Pop suggested.

"The cannon!" I gasped. "What if *Gee* is *in* the cannon?"

Paul was speaking again, a ladies-and-gentlemen-hold-on-to-your-hats kind of announcement, but Leo was raising such a fuss now that attention in our neighborhood was going to him. Paul began glancing our way in annoyance.

"Pop!" I said. "What if Leo—?"

Pop said quickly, "Let the dog go, Howard. Let him go."

The dog went, trailing his leash, straight into the arena.

Everything stopped: even the weather seemed to hold its breath as Leo churned up the sawdust, pelted right by the platform with the cannon, and skidded to a stop at the bottom of the tower. Then he raised his head, and out of his throat came the truest, loudest, most honest-to-dog *barking* I've ever heard.

I started to duck under the rail, but Pop put a hand on my shoulder to stop me. I could feel the hand shaking. "My job," he said. Then he walked down to an opening in the barrier and right out into the arena like the lone sheriff of Dodge. A bolt of lightning cracked over our heads, and the thunder rumbled.

There were suddenly two people on the cannon platform, Paul and another guy in a black skintight outfit—his brother. They were having an agitated conversation. "Where did Tim come from?" I whispered.

"From inside the cannon," Howard whispered back—even though there was no need to keep it down, with conversations starting to buzz all around us. "I saw him crawl out the other end."

Pop had reached the foot of the tower, where Leo was still exercising his lungs and two fair officials were trying to pull him away. Pop exchanged a few words with them, and they stepped aside as he started to climb the steel ladder. I wasn't sure how far up he could make himself go—especially with a couple of fractured ribs—but I noticed he didn't look down. A couple of feet from the top, he paused, and I could hear the tiniest scratch of his voice, calling Gee's name. I stepped out into the arena, and Howard followed me. *Gee's got to be there,* I thought. *Please let him be there.* Another blast of wind shook the stands, throwing cold rain in my face.

The crowd murmured at a movement on the top of the tower: a spot of red that turned into a little boy's T-shirt. "Hey, look!" Howard said beside me.

Suddenly unable to speak—or look—I had to turn around and hug him hard, which surprised him so much he didn't dare say anything more.

After a minute, Gee crawled slowly over the edge of the tower platform, turned around, and clung to Pop's neck. With his left arm around him, Pop began the climb down, one step at a time.

Don't worry about SuperSizing or maximizing or advantagizing your life. Just be there for it.

—Veronica Sparks

Before things get too sticky around here, I'd better say that Cannonball Paul was *really* ticked off. When Pop finally set foot on solid ground again, Paul was right there, and by the time Howard and I ran up, he was launched. His point was hard to dispute. We'd ruined his only chance for an exhibition shoot—now that the rain was pelting down and the stands were clearing out fast.

But did he expect Pop to just wait calmly for a dummy to fly over the tower before checking to see if Gee was there? Tim, who arrived about the same time Howard and I did, took our side. "Come on, man, this is that kid they were looking for. If it was your kid, would you wait? Even for a second?"

All that time my grandfather held on to Gee, and vice versa, while Leo danced for joy. Finally, Pop reached into his shirt pocket for one of his business cards. "Call me— we'll settle up later." Then he just walked away and left Paul sputtering behind him.

I found myself holding on to my brother's shoe. Gee seemed more-than-usually shook up, but he gave me a small, sickly smile around the thumb in his mouth, so I figured he'd be all right. He'd better, with all the explaining he had to do. Leo pranced beside us making *woof-woof* sounds, like he had warmed up to the barking business, but Pop snapped at him to shut up, and he mostly did.

"What now, Mr. Hazeltine?" Howard asked. We were all drenched.

Pop looked kind of shook himself, as if he couldn't believe what he had just done in front of all those people. "Guess we can all squeeze back in your truck and hit the road. You can stay with us in the Coachman tonight, if your mother—"

At that minute an "Official Staff" person stopped us. "Sir? Mr. Hazeltine? This is the boy you were looking for, right?" We all nodded. "Great. We'll alert the highway patrol. But in the meantime, here's somebody who wants to see you."

He gestured toward a lighted picnic shelter where so many people had taken refuge I couldn't tell which one he meant. My eyes passed right over the lady in the wheelchair, but Gee, squirming around in Pop's arms, shouted, "Mama!"

More stickiness, which I will skip over—use your imagination. It wasn't the highway patrol who alerted our mother, it was Becki the convenience-store clerk, who turned over my card and saw my number on the front. Smart of me, right? Mama then frantically called the Kansas Highway Department, and kept getting transferred, until she finally got hold of Officer Hadley, who told her where we were. He also gave her Howard's cell number, but she didn't get an answer when she called it because Howard's battery had run down. Then she called Lyddie, who came right over, and they set off for Kansas after stopping at the medical supply to rent the wheelchair. They'd just arrived, after six hours on the road. "That's the most gut-wrenching trip I've ever made," Lyddie said cheerfully. "You'd better not do this again, Gee."

Gee, curled up like a rock in Mama's lap, still wasn't talking.

The rain settled into a steady patter and most of the fair-goers under the shelter decided to call it a night. With the additions to our party, and Mama, for one, at the end of her endurance, Pop gave up his idea of Howard driving us back to the Coachman. I guessed he was pretty much at the end of his endurance, too, though he wouldn't admit it. So the adults among us decided to rent a motel room—but since Pop was paying for it, we only rented one.

Fortunately, it was a suite, with a separate bedroom and a foldout sofa. Pop took the sofa, and Howard took the floor. Gee started out with Pop, but he's a very squirmy sleeper, which is why he ended up on the floor, too. Mama and Lyddie got the queen-size bed, and I sacked out with some pillows on the recliner.

But before that, we had to order pizza and deprogram after a very packed day: the same day, remember, that began with Pop installing an alternator in the desolate wilderness of the Chalk Pyramids. Between then and now, we'd been shuffled and reshuffled and wrung through the wringer of human emotion, all because of our smallest and youngest person. Who finally talked.

Just like I suspected, he'd stowed away on the

Cannonball trailer back at the truck plaza—after running almost smack-dab into it when he turned the corner of the full-service restaurant. Luck was with him, if you want to call it that, because the side door was unlocked. Once he was inside, he was so overwhelmed to be among Cannon-ball Paul's stuff, including that silver suit spread across one of the beds, that he didn't start having second thoughts about the wisdom of this plan until someone locked the door from outside and second thoughts wouldn't have done any good anyway.

Once they were on the highway and rolling like gang-busters, Gee panicked and pounded on the door, to no avail. After he realized how unavailing panic was, he did something unusual: he sat down and thought about his sit-uation. If he turned himself in now, Pop would be furious and not only would Gee never see Cannonball Paul, he might never see Pop again. So he decided to be calm, enjoy the ride, and call home as soon as he had a chance so peo-ple could stop worrying.

It wasn't until they reached the campground that he came up with the second part of the plan. After the truck had parked and Gee realized where they were, he hid him-self in one of the storage bins. When the brothers came in for lunch, he overheard bits and pieces of the conversation and learned about the exhibition shoot. But didn't catch the part about a dummy being shot, not Paul. So at the first opportunity, Gee slipped out of the trailer and hiked across the field to the fairground, slipping in without much trou-ble because he's a champion slipper.

That's why the patrolmen didn't find him in Paul's

trailer—he wasn't there. He was touring the fair, scrounging bits of food that people had left on their plates ("Oh, Gee," Mama sighed) and wishing he had enough money for the Scrambler—all with no idea that every gas-station attendant and convenience-store clerk and law-enforcement officer in Kansas was looking for him. He did use the dollar in his pocket to call home—nice thought, but bad timing because Mama had already left with Lyddie.

After scoping out the arena where the shoot was going to be, he decided to get in place well ahead of time—and what better place than the tower Paul would be flying over? He caught the last of a livestock show, then waited through the cleanup. After the maintenance people were gone, he darted out and scurried up the side of the tower, praying nobody would see him, because the place was never entirely empty.

"But, Gee," I interrupted, "didn't you learn *anything* from Big Brutus?"

"Uh-huh." He was bouncing up and down on the sofa. "I knew I'd have a hard time getting down. But if I just stood up and yelled loud enough after the shoot, somebody'd come and get me."

Not bad, I thought, for Gee. But the thunder and lightning he didn't count on, so all the time Paul was going through his opening spiel, Gee was huddled on top of the tower trying to keep from hollering for help ("Poor baby," murmured Lyddie). Then he heard a dog bark, and the rest is history.

In the silence that followed his story, I listened to the

steady patter of rain outside and thought about what Gee had done. Granted, the whole idea wasn't very smart. But he'd shown a never-before-seen ability to plan and carry out a short-term goal. Pop must have been thinking the same thing, because he finally said, "Don't ever let anybody tell you you're stupid, Gee."

My brother blinked in surprise. "I don't. I usually pop 'em one."

It's hard enough living in a house with three people and one bathroom, but imagine the traffic jam the next morning with six. Mama stayed out of it, and Gee slept in, but the rest of us were up and stirring by seven. Pop and Howard were going back to the truck stop to get the RV, and Lyddie decided to go with them—to "keep Jack company on the way back" was the way she put it. Looked like Jack had won another middle-aged lady's heart.

I got up, too, mostly to tell Howard good-bye. "I hope you smooth things over with your parents," I said as we stood by his pickup, waiting for the adults to come out.

"Not a problem. They can't do without me." He smiled, and all of a sudden things got awkward. "Think you might come back sometime? Even though you don't like Kansas very much?"

"Who said I didn't like Kansas?" The more I saw, the more I liked: soaring sky, wide plains, the unexpectedness of Big Brutus and the Chalk Pyramids and the World's Largest Hand-Dug Well, which I now wanted to see. The state might look flat and uninteresting, but all kinds of cool things hunkered down waiting to be found. "I *love* Kansas."

He looked kind of embarrassed, as if I'd said I loved *him*. So I decided to embarrass him a little more, and gave him a great big hug. "By the way, thanks for everything. You're my hero."

"Right." He might have squeezed me back before breaking away—hard to tell. "You should see Rock City. It's this field full of huge boulders that look like great big balls of twine. And then there's this *real* ball of twine in Cawker City? Biggest in the world." He bent down to scratch Leo's ears. "Be good, big guy. And if they decide they can't keep you, come on back."

Pop offered to drive the pickup, but Howard said he could manage. I guess he couldn't wait to charge onto the interstate again. When he pulled out, with Pop and Lyddie squeezed into the cab, I yelled, "Call me sometime!" then stood on the curb and waved until that blue-and-white pickup was all the way out of sight.

After that, I curled up in bed with Mama and we just talked. It's not often we get to do that, with her work and all the demands of home—not to mention the demands of Gee. But he was still sacked out on the living room floor, and in the stillness of the morning we talked and talked, and I told her everything I could remember about the trip, even the scary parts. She laughed, she cried, she exclaimed, "Oh no!"

Finally, she asked, "So what do you think? Are you glad you went? Did you get what you were hoping for?"

My mixed feelings from yesterday came back to me— when I was furious with Pop and furious with Gee, kind of homesick but at the same time not ready to go back. "Glad

I went, for sure," was my final answer. "Whether I got what I was hoping for . . ."

What *was* I hoping for? I'd met my short-term goals, except for organizing better. With Gee around, chaos trumped organization every time. But there seemed to be more to it than just meeting goals. Maybe I'd been wind-prospecting like Pop, chasing something that couldn't be caught. Trying to wrap it up for Mama, all I could say was, "Ask me in a week."

Lyddie had to go home that day to see her granddaughter's dance recital, and Mama's knee was crying for its old home on the couch. I kind of assumed that when they left for Missouri, Gee and I would be in the back seat of Lyddie's Buick. But later that morning, when the Coachman had returned and Mama told Gee to get his stuff out of it, Pop asked, "What for?"

"Well, to go home," Mama said, looking puzzled.

"They're not going home until tomorrow. I'll bring them." Everybody in the room stopped what they were doing to look at him. "Well, Gee hasn't seen Cannonball Paul do his shoot yet. That's not until one, so—"

Gee yelled and threw himself at Pop, which wasn't the way to get on the man's good side, but Gee's a slow learner. Mama hobbled up on her crutches, eyes gleaming. "Oh, Dad."

He put an arm around her shoulders and gave her a squeeze, which wasn't easy with all that aluminum between them. "Can we see Rock City?" I asked. "It's this field of huge round boulders that look kind of like big balls of

twine, out in the middle of—"

"Maybe," he said, and to Mama he added, "I'll bring 'em back sometime tomorrow."

As she nodded, sniffling, a knock on the door startled us all.

I answered it.

There was a guy in jeans and a T-shirt standing on the sidewalk, looking kind of familiar, and kind of nervous. As he shifted light as a dancer from one foot to the other, I recognized him in a gulp: Cannonball Paul! With his blond hair down in his face instead of combed back, he looked a lot younger. And, frankly, kind of ordinary.

"Hi," he said, then stepped back and motioned me to follow. "Look, I don't have much time. It took a while to find you, and I've got to get back soon. I just wanted to say, I'm sorry for yesterday. What I said. Thinking it over, I don't blame you for anything." I just gaped at him. "So. To make it up, I wanted to invite you all to the shoot today." He reached into his pocket and pulled out a handful of those blue passes.

I started making thank-you noises, which he waved away. "One more thing. Tonight, I plan on renting a little Cessna two-seater—airplane, that is—to fly up during the fireworks. Tim doesn't want to go because he signed up for a weight-lifting competition. So I was thinking—if the boy wants to fly, I'll take him."

My thank-you noises changed to this-is-going-too-fast-for-me noises. "What—when—?"

He took another step back. "You guys talk it over and

tell me after the shoot what you decided. One o'clock, in the arena. Catch you then." With another wave, he bounded off the curb and into his white truck, burning a little rubber when he backed away. It all happened so fast I could barely believe he'd been there, except for the blue passes in my hand.

"Who was that?" Lyddie asked when I went back inside.

My news raised an uproar, with Gee begging and whining, Mom doubting she'd ever let her little boy go up in a tin can with a stranger, and Lyddie saying, "But it's the chance of a lifetime!"

Exactly, I thought. If it was me, I'd be all over it, but nobody asked me. Gee was the squeaky wheel who got the grease in this family. Biting my lip, I glanced at Pop, who looked back but didn't say anything.

Finally, Mama said, "Since I won't be here, I'll leave it to you, Dad. I'm probably better off not knowing till it's over anyway."

No matter how hard Gee pressed him, Pop wouldn't commit to yes or no, and he still hadn't said when the ladies left at eleven. After hugs all around, like we weren't going to see each other the very next day, Lyddie extended an invitation: "If you get back by dinnertime tomorrow, Jack, come on over. I'll throw some steaks on the grill." It was an eye-rolling moment, but I restrained myself.

With everything else that had happened, the actual Cannonball shoot—Paul blasting straight as an arrow from the mouth of the big white gun, sailing over the tower, and landing dead center in the net—was almost an anticlimax. Though Gee yelled loud enough to be a whole cheering section by himself.

For myself, I'll admit to feeling a little resentful. Whatever Pop decided about Paul's invitation, it bothered me how much life still revolved around Gee—what he needed, what he did, what he caused. This trip had turned out to be all about *him*. Don't get me wrong: my brother's appearance on the top of the tower the night before was the biggest relief of my life.

But doesn't that kind of prove my point?

After the crowd in the arena had thinned out, we went down for a demo. Tim showed us the cannon and explained a little of its operation (without giving away the secret, of course) and told us why he had to be inside to pull the trigger that shot Paul. The barrel of the gun didn't look big enough for one man, let alone two.

At the first long pause, Pop said, "About your invitation. I appreciate it, but I don't see any point in rewarding Gee for worrying the daylights out of all of us."

Gee gulped, as though gearing up for a monster-whine, but he stood down when Pop looked warningly at him.

"However," my grandfather went on, "if you're still willing to take somebody, I suggest you take Ronnie."

Believe the unbelievable.

—Me

How did he know? How, in the whirl of our post-Gee-stress disorder, had he noticed that if anybody should go on an evening airplane ride through the fireworks, it was me?

Paul didn't have any problem with it. Gee did, at first, but a couple of rides on the Scrambler made him see reason—funny that scrambling his brain turns out to be the best thing for it, sometimes. The rest of that afternoon was the classic Day Out with Grandpa that Mama had hoped for: cotton candy, corn dogs, and midway rides, with Pop footing the bill and only refusing about half of Gee's requests.

Paul had told us to be at the airport no later than eight, so he could take off by eight-thirty. To me it felt like ages since we'd been in the Coachman, Gee nodding in the dinette seat and me in my luxury swivel chair on the passenger side. But of course, it was only a little over twenty-four hours. My head was full of things to say as we drove toward the lowering sun, but they all felt too heavy for the moment. Except for, "Thanks, Pop."

"Hmmm?" He seemed kind of preoccupied.

"Thanks for speaking up for me about the plane ride. I know it's some trouble, hauling me out here, but—"

"Minor trouble, comparatively."

He probably meant, compared to everything else he'd

been through on this trip. "Well, anyway . . . I'm sorry you lost all this time on the job and—"

"I'll make it up." Without you kids, he might have added, but didn't.

"Mama seems to think you've made up for a lot. Probably enough to stay away for the next two years."

I didn't mean to sound sarcastic, but it might have come out that way. After a minute, he sighed. "Ronnie."

"Yes, sir?"

"I should've been coming around to see y'all more often. Your mother's right—Gee needs a firm hand and I can help with that. And you—" I held my breath, wondering what I needed. "You've got an interesting life ahead. I'd like to be around for more of it."

Breathing again, I asked, "So you're moving to Partly?"

He just snorted at that. Then he smiled. "If I did, there's a lady in Muleshoe, Texas, who'd really miss me. . . ."

Paul's white truck was in the airport lot when we arrived, and shortly after, Paul came out of the small white building with a clipboard in hand. He waved at us but kept on walking out to the airfield, where a dozen or so small planes were waiting in a row.

He stopped at the smallest, a sporty yellow-and-white job with wings across the top. As we walked up, he was checking the propeller and wheels and a lot of other parts I couldn't name, while consulting the laminated list on his clipboard. Gee yelled, "Hi, Paul!"

Not one to carry a grudge, Paul looked up and smiled. "Hi, guys. I'll be ready in about fifteen minutes."

There wasn't much to do while he inspected the cockpit. Pop asked a few questions, and kept Gee from asking more questions, but I just stood aside and let the evening kind of soak in. After last night's heavy rain, the day had been steamy, but a fresh breeze was blowing busily out of the west, carrying a scent of cut grass and damp soil. The haze in the air turned gold, smudging the sunset to a deep yellow. Lights twinkled on the plains that stretched out all around us, and I imagined that once in the sky, I could see till Sunday.

Paul stepped down from the cockpit doorway, where he'd been checking the fuel gauge on the wing. "That's it. Climb aboard—what was your name again?"

"Veronica," I said, before anyone could say different.

"That's pretty. Climb on board, Veronica, and I'll get your grandfather to move the chocks out from under the wheels."

Inside, the plane seemed no bigger than a tin can, as my mother had said, with very thin walls. I shivered, in spite of myself.

Paul hoisted himself up beside me, and the whole plane rocked with his weight. The cockpit was so small I could have puked in his lap. "Ever flown before?" he asked me.

"No."

"Once we get started, it'll be pretty noisy, so speak now if you're having second thoughts."

"No way!"

"That's the spirit." He buckled his seat belt and started

throwing little switches on the dashboard—if that's what you call it on a plane. "My first time was a little scary."

"Even compared to getting shot out of a cannon?"

"Oh, that? Nothing to it. *This* is a kick. Expensive, though. Someday I'll get my own plane, close to where I live." He snapped a pair of headphones over his ears, picked up the microphone by his knee, and told Hays Traffic that he was about to depart.

"Where do you live?" I'd had the idea he was as footloose as Pop, with no address more permanent than a trailer park.

"Just bought a place last year." Paul opened his window, shouted, "Clear props!" and closed it again. "Nice little acreage, a few miles outside of a little town called Partly, Missouri."

My jaw dropped, and the propeller roared. We taxied toward the end of the runway. When I found my voice, I yelled, "Don't tell Gee!"

"WHAT?" he yelled back. I just waved a hand, indicating I'd tell him later. Talk about surprises! If Gee knew, we'd never hear the end of it. Come to think of it, if Paul knew, he might be tempted to move. Better it be my own little secret for now.

Heading down the runway, I surprised myself by having second thoughts. The plane rattled like a tray of silverware in an earthquake, and everything in it was rattling right along, including my stomach. Paul tilted the steering-wheel thingy, and like Howard on the interstate ramp, I clenched my teeth and held on as we picked up speed. The plane shook harder and harder, until it suddenly gave a little hop and I felt the wheels leave the ground. The rattling cut by half as we angled into the sky. "Wow!" I shouted.

Paul looked over and grinned. We circled the field, wagging our wings, and there was a tiny Pop, waving, while a tiny Gee spun himself in circles with his arms spread wide. Beyond the airfield, big round bales of hay in the fields looked like buttons, and the lights of Hays blazed like a Christmas pageant. We buzzed the highway, looped around the courthouse, and headed for the fairgrounds as the last glow of sunset faded from the sky.

I was staring at the festival of neon and the bright bangle of the Ferris wheel when Paul pointed off to my right. A silvery streak gleamed against the dark, then exploded in a shower of green and blue. Paul shouted something, and I just nodded, smiling so hard my cheeks hurt—*let's go!*

This is what I came for, I thought. *This is what I'm taking back with me, and it's something I couldn't have expected or planned.* Who'd have thought I could experience this, out in the middle of—

But wait a minute. There is no *no*where. Every place you are is the middle of somewhere.

Swooping in a glorious curve that tilted us to the right, Paul steadied the wings just as another canister exploded. And we flew straight for its golden, blooming, billowing heart.